Fire in the Spirit

A Story of St. Hild and St. Æthelthryth

by Valerie Tupling Ansdell

◆ FriesenPress

Suite 300 - 990 Fort St
Victoria, BC, V8V 3K2
Canada

www.friesenpress.com

Copyright © 2017 by Valerie Tupling Ansdell
First Edition — 2017

All rights reserved.

No part of this publication may be reproduced in any form, or by any means, electronic or mechanical, including photocopying, recording, or any information browsing, storage, or retrieval system, without permission in writing from FriesenPress.

ISBN
978-1-4602-9839-8 (Hardcover)
978-1-4602-9840-4 (Paperback)
978-1-4602-9841-1 (eBook)

1. FICTION, HISTORICAL

Distributed to the trade by The Ingram Book Company

To Maggie
a friend for the ages

TABLE OF CONTENTS

Author's Foreword ix
An Introduction to Seventh-Century Anglo-Saxon Britain xiii
A Further Note on Time xxi

THE BEGINNING
Chapter One 1
Chapter Two 10
Chapter Three 22
Chapter Four 30
Chapter Five 37
Chapter Six 44
Chapter Seven 50

THE MIDDLE YEARS
Letter One 56
Letter Two 59
Letter Three 62
Letter Four 65
Letter Five 68
Letter Six 70
Letter Seven 73
Letter Eight 75

THE GATHERING
Chapter Eight 78
Chapter Nine 82
Chapter Ten 88
Chapter Eleven 92
Chapter Twelve 94
Chapter Thirteen 100

THE DESPERATE YEARS
Letter Nine 108
Letter Ten 110

Letter Eleven 114
Letter Twelve 117
Letter Thirteen 119

FLIGHT FROM NORTHUMBRIA
Chapter Fourteen 124

THE COVENANT FULFILLED
Letter Fourteen 138
Letter Fifteen 141
Letter Sixteen 144
Letter Seventeen 147
Letter Eighteen 150

APPENDIX
St. Hild of Whitby 154
St. Etheldreda of Ely 155
Ecgfrith, King of Northumbria 670–685 157
Saint Wilfrid c. 634–709 159
St. Æbba of Coldingham 161
Eanflæd and Ælfflæd 163
Endnote Abbreviations for Frequently Cited Sources 165
Endnotes 166
Bibliography 182

The Heptarchy of 7th Century Anglo-Saxon Britain

- ● with place name - denotes settlements relevant to the story of Etheldreda and Hild.
- ● without place name - denotes other settlements and towns in the 7th century.
- − − − denotes the old Roman roads.

Sussex, Wessex & Essex are more recent names for the old kingdoms of the South, West & East Saxons.

Author's Foreword

When I was reading Medieval English Literature with Dr. Sarah Keefer at Trent University in the 1990s, I was introduced to a different understanding of the Anglo-Saxons and their ways of thinking and being. Particularly intriguing was the role that noble women played in the culture of the 7th century.

The popular perception of Anglo-Saxon Britain is that of a barbaric and lawless rampaging horde, unmarked by any signs of civilization. That makes for good movies and television, I suppose, however it isn't a very balanced picture.

This book is about an evolution of thought and belief in the 7th century — the time of "the great conversion" as it is sometimes called. The gradual spread of Christianity across the kingdoms of Britain changed everything.

Anyone researching women in 7th century Anglo-Saxon Britain soon discovers two truths. The first is that factual information is very scarce and mostly unreliable. The second is that all roads lead to Bede.

Monk, historian, prolific author, teacher, scientist, poet, and mathematician, the Venerable Bede was a true Renaissance man centuries before the term was invented.

Bede spent his life (c. 673–735) in a Northumbrian monastery where he was free to pursue his many interests. Although he wrote numerous books on various subjects, the one most relevant to us and the story that follows is his *History of the English Church and People (Historia ecclesiastica gentis Anglorum)* completed in 731 and cited numerous times throughout the endnotes as *HE*. Bede's texts are invaluable to students of the early Anglo-Saxon period as he strives to illuminate the beliefs and mindsets of a nation in the throes of abandoning the old ways and struggling to understand the nature of the Christian God.

While researching this book, I have discovered that were it not for Bede, information about the activities of women during the 7th century and before would be scant indeed. Two women he seemed to particularly admire are the protagonists in the story that follows. I am personally grateful to him for this.

Another ancient scholar whose work I have cited frequently is the anonymous monk (or monks) of Ely who, in the 12th century, compiled an ambitious historical work called the *Liber Eliensis (Book of Ely)*. I feel it is incumbent upon me to include here a caveat regarding the dependability of the information in this work.

The writer of the *Liber* embarked on his project with a clear political agenda. In his time, the monasteries were embroiled in disputes with King Stephen regarding ownership of monastery lands. The writer was determined to impress upon the powerful religious and secular leaders of the day the importance of the Ely monastery and its religious community. Hagiography, the biographical study of the lives of saints, was a valuable tool in his argument and he used it effectively with regard to St. Æthelthryth, one of the protagonists in the following story. St. Æthelthryth is also known as St. Audrey and, prior to sainthood, as Etheldreda.

Although many of the claims in the *Liber* are suspect or patently untrue, some of the stories surrounding Etheldreda's adventures have been included in this book because they help to illuminate the way in which she was perceived by future historians. Whether or not they actually happened remains to be proved, but who is to say now that the miracles she experienced were not true. Oddly enough, Bede, who loved a good miracle, mentions neither in his writings about Etheldreda.

The historian, Antonia Gransden, has said of the *Liber* that it is "valuable for general history" but qualifies this by writing that "the whole lacks unity and has errors and confusing repetitions." (*Historical Writing in England c. 550 to c. 1307*, London: Routledge & Kegan Paul, 1974, 270)

There is no doubt that fundamental errors abound in the *Liber*. However, given the gaps in information and our dependence upon who is telling the story, it must be said that contradictions will constantly bedevil anyone attempting to write about the early Anglo-Saxon era.

If, as a reader, you feel your understanding of 7th century Britain is vague, blurry or non-existent, I would encourage you to read through the introduction before jumping right into the story. Although it is a very brief overview, it is meant to offer the reader some clarity of vision regarding the time period and the background against which the story of Hild and Etheldreda is set.

I would also encourage you to spend some time with the endnotes as they contain many tidbits of information which will undoubtedly help to deepen your understanding of the seventh century in Britain and the characters who stride through the pages of the story of St. Hild and St. Æthelthryth.

Valerie Tupling Ansdell, 2016

An Introduction to Seventh-Century Anglo-Saxon Britain

Historians tell us that when the Roman legions withdrew from Britain in the first half of the fifth century of the Common Era,[1] the remaining Roman Britons found themselves overwhelmed by native tribes such as the Picts and the Scots. Barbarian Germanic tribes from Europe were invited into Britain as mercenaries to help subdue the native tribes.[2]

From the standpoint of the Roman Britons, this turned out to be an unwise decision. Before long, the mercenaries — mainly Angles from the south of the Danish peninsula, Saxons from areas now known as northern Germany and Holland, and Jutes from Jutland — discovered that they liked this verdant new country. They began dividing it up amongst themselves through wars and political alliances. Thus, the Roman Britons had neatly exchanged one enemy for another.

By the seventh century, the country we now know as England had been roughly divided into seven political entities through colonization by the descendants of the earlier mercenary warriors. Later, historians of the early twelfth century would come to regard the seven kingdoms — Kent, Sussex, Essex, Wessex, East Anglia, Mercia, and Northumbria — as the Heptarchy.[3]

With the exception of a few peaceful interludes, war was waged incessantly among the early tribes who settled these areas during the fifth, sixth, and seventh centuries. Consequently, the boundaries of the seven kingdoms were frequently in flux, ebbing and flowing according to victories and defeats.

These were violent, bloodthirsty times. Countrysides were ravaged, homes and villages pillaged and burned, innocents scourged and slaughtered or enslaved. Each warrior ruler was consumed by greed for land and power.

This is not to suggest that these warrior tribes were entirely lawless or without any governing influences. When they migrated from continental Europe to Britain, the Angles, Saxons, and Jutes carried with them their ancestral political and cultural traditions of kingship, kinship, feud, and wergild. Dr. Barbara Yorke has this to say about Anglo-Saxon kingship:

> Kings and kingship were the dominant political organization in England during the Anglo-Saxon period. The foundation myths which survive for some Anglo-Saxon kingdoms depict their founders as military leaders who won their kingdoms by defeating British rulers in battle in the late fifth and sixth centuries. Whatever the truth of these accounts, warleadership can be seen to be a major activity of kings in the seventh and eighth

centuries and a major source of revenue through the collection of tribute. (Yorke, *BE*, 271)

Kings were also responsible for the dispossessed and those without kin group, such as "foreigners, foundlings, ecclesiastics, and emancipated slaves." (Hough, *BE*, 273) Illegitimate children disowned by their fathers also fit this category.

Kings rarely acted alone, as they were closely counseled by their Witan or chief men regarding all matters of duty, honour, and sovereignty. The role of kinship is explained as

> a central part in the structural framework of Anglo-Saxon society. The maintenance of law and order depended to a large extent on the collective responsibility of individual kindreds for the safety and good conduct of their members; and the rights and obligations of kinship groups feature prominently in the laws. It was the duty of the kindred to seek justice for a member who was killed or injured either by prosecuting a feud or by exacting the appropriate financial compensation: cf wergild.[4] Conversely, they were required to ensure that an accused member appeared to answer the charge. If convicted, a member could expect food and support from the kindred while in prison as well as assistance in meeting the prescribed penalty; but no aid would be given to an outlaw.[5] A woman's interest continued to be safeguarded after marriage by her own kindred, and

> the paternal kin were responsible for administering the property of orphaned minors. (Hough, BE, 272)

At the end of the sixth century, the laws governing this emergent society were set down by Æthelberht I (d. 616), King of Kent and third Bretwalda[6] who was also the first Anglo-Saxon king to convert to Christianity. Æthelberht's system of laws is thought to be one of the first documents ever written down in the English vernacular.[7]

As in all societies, religion was an integral part of Anglo-Saxon culture. Christianity had flourished sporadically and in geographic pockets during the Roman occupation. By the time the Angles, Saxons, and Jutes arrived in Britain, only vestiges of the new religion remained and most of the native tribes continued to worship the old gods. The newcomers, who were called pagan by the few remaining scattered Christians, apparently worshipped a pantheon of Germanic gods.

According to Stenton:

> The heathen background of Old English history is impenetrably vague…the general stock of knowledge about Germanic paganism…is indefinite at almost every crucial point, it is often coloured by scriptural reminiscence, and it affords no more than the faintest of clues to the nature of the beliefs which lay behind observances. (96)[8]

The significant point is that heathenism was alive and well in early Anglo-Saxon England when Christianity was reintroduced[9] with renewed vigour during the sixth century. (Stenton. 102)

On the eve of Pentecost, 12th of May in the year 563, Columba, an Irish monk, and his twelve companions landed on the island of Iona on the west coast of present-day Scotland with evangelism on their minds.

This event signalled the beginning of the conversion of the Picts and other northern tribes into the Celtic tradition of Christianity. By preaching and by example, Columba and his followers exerted widespread influence throughout Pictland and the Northumbrian kingdom. They were able to claim mass conversions among the people. Columba died in June of 597, leaving behind him many disciples who were dedicated to spreading Celtic Christianity throughout all Britain.

Coincidentally, that same spring of 597 heralded the arrival from Rome of Augustine who landed on the island of Thanet off the coast of Kent in southern England. Augustine and his group of forty Roman monks had been dispatched to Britain by Pope Gregory the Great with the specific mission of rescuing Christianity in what had by this time become a predominantly pagan land. They were welcomed by Bertha, the Frankish wife of Æthelberht I (the law-maker mentioned previously), who was herself already a Christian. When Augustine died somewhere between 604 and 609, he had consecrated several bishops throughout the land to carry on the work of spreading the Christian faith.[10]

The course of the mass conversion of Britain did not run smoothly at the outset. When kings were persuaded to be baptized, their people usually followed en masse.

When a king lapsed into the old religion, his people generally followed suit. Gradually, the new religion took a firmer hold on the minds and hearts of the Anglo-Saxons. However, there were many small and large differences in the theology and practice of Christianity rooted in the Celtic tradition and that of the Romans. These stumbling blocks led to numerous disputes over the correctness of belief and the timing of the liturgical year.[11]

The political, cultural and religious world of the early Anglo-Saxons was a mysterious concoction of ancient traditions blended with emergent ideas and a new religion. This brief glimpse is meant merely to provide the reader with some context and to serve as the background against which two of the most remarkable and complex women of the seventh century lived out their lives.

Hild, or St. Hilda, was a minor member of the Northumbrian royal family and, therefore, exposed to both Celtic influences and Roman as this tradition edged northward. Etheldreda, variously known as St. Æthelthryth or St. Audrey, was a princess of the royal house of East Anglia and subject for the most part to Roman tradition. It is possible to say that she may have known something of the lifestyle and Celtic ideas of the Irish monk, Fursey, who maintained a hermitage in East Anglia under royal patronage.[12] Hild was a devoted and steadfast mother of the fledgling church, and Etheldreda was a zealot obsessed with her own chastity and her place in the church as a bride of Christ. Both women brought strength of character, wisdom, intelligence, passion, and devotion to their lives lived out in the male-dominated warrior society of seventh-century Anglo-Saxon England.

Hild and Etheldreda were members of the noble or royal class and, as such, were in the top two percent of the citizenry. Unfortunately, the other ninety-eight percent of women lived dreary lives of drudgery and squalor, often sharing their homes with the animals that comprised part of their livelihood. Many of them worked long days in the field, stopping only occasionally to give birth to another mouth to feed. But even these peasant women were a class above female slaves who had no rights under the law and whose lives depended precariously on the whims of their masters.

Any attempt to illuminate the early Anglo-Saxon period should be accompanied by a cautionary note. Because the historical sources are undependable and sporadic, cited dates are often off by a year or even a decade. Genealogies are notoriously confusing, as they have had to be reconstructed from material containing significant gaps and from sources containing many spelling variations of individuals' names. A further problem for works about women is that the chroniclers closest in chronological time, mostly monks, royal scribes, and itinerant poets, were not much interested in women's activities since they were deemed not to be particularly heroic or historic.

The fact that the compilers of the Parker Chronicle (A) and the Laud Chronicle (E) would chose to record the date that Etheldreda founded her monastery at Ely (673) and the death dates of both Hild (680) and Etheldreda, or St. Æthelthryth, (679) demonstrates the impact they must have had on their society at that time.[13]

So taken was the Venerable Bede with Etheldreda's religious heroics he dedicated two chapters to her (*HE*,

IV: xix, xx). The first details her life in the church, and the second is a hymn of praise to this "Holy Virgin". Bede also devotes a long chapter to the life and death of Abbess Hilda in which he notes that, "Kings and princes, as occasion offered, asked and received her advice." (*HE*, IV: xxiii)

Much of what follows, therefore, is a combination of historical record, traditional and religious lore, and finally, when the gaps cannot be closed by any other method, educated supposition.

A Further Note on Time

With the advent of Christianity in Anglo-Saxon England, the Old Saxon calendar, which was based on lunar cycles and agricultural concerns, gradually gave way to the Julian calendar whose month names are the ones still in use today. In the Julian system, the new year began in March, which explains why the months of September, October, November, and December have the Latin prefixes of the seventh, eighth, ninth, and tenth months. In the text that follows, where dates are required, I have used the Julian calendar for the reader's ease of comprehension. However, in the historical time that the text is set, the agricultural society of Anglo-Saxon England would be continuing to employ the Old Saxon calendar for planting time, harvest, and other traditional non-Christian agricultural celebrations.

THE BEGINNING

Rendlesham, East Anglia, Britain

Late summer in the year of our Lord 647

Chapter One

I am crouched on my little wooden stool in my chamber, examining my feet. They seem such odd things. I wonder how God decided this is what feet should look like. Bishop Felix tells me that the ways of God are mysterious and not for us mere mortals to understand. But I am Etheldreda, daughter of Anna, the king of East Anglia, and I have made it my mission to try to understand the mind of God.

Hoof beats pounding on the hard-packed mud of the village road disturb my thoughts. They clatter on the cobbles of the great hall's[14] courtyard. Through my tiny window slit, I watch the messenger leap from his horse. He pounds on the massive wooden double doors with the hammer side of his axe. My heart pounds with the same beat. Is he bringing the message that we all fear? Is he coming to report that the rampaging warlord, Penda of Mercia, has turned his snarling face toward East Anglia again? Is he coming to tell my father that the Mercian raiders are once more scourging the countryside and butchering our people?

The little opening in the small door embedded in one of the big doors slides back, and I hear Uvid, my father's steward, demand to know who is making such a racket.

"I come in peace with a message for King Anna," the rider announces. A great breath of relief escapes me.

"Leave your weapons with your horse," instructs Uvid. "I will send a stable boy to fetch them."

When the messenger complies, Uvid opens the small door and ushers him in. I scurry quickly over to the door of my chamber in time to see him stride into the great hall of Rendlesham. Most of my father's household guards[15] still sprawl on the filthy rushes, snorting like pigs after the previous night's carousing.

Father emerges from his room, his cloak hastily thrown over his sleeping shirt. The messenger quickly sinks to the smooth stone floor and stays there till my father waves his hand for him to rise.

They speak together in soft tones and even my excellent ears can not make out the words. After a few moments, my father nods and waves the messenger toward the kitchens, where Berga will no doubt satisfy his belly. He then circles the room, nudging the sleeping men with his bare foot.

"Get up, y'craven louts!" he shouts with more affection than annoyance. "Get your stenchy bodies out of here. We are to have a visitor, and I would have this hall scoured and readied."

A visitor!

My belly jumps at the news though I have no idea who the visitor might be. It must be a person of some import though, because father begins barking orders at the hall servants. Then straightaway he takes himself off to the kitchens, still in his nightclothes.

I creep back into my chamber and sit again on the small stool by my window slit. After a few minutes, horse and rider burst from the stable yard. They disappear far away down the road from whence they came. By now, my servant girl, who sleeps on a straw pallet in the corner of my chamber, is awake and rubbing her eyes.

"Get a move on, Freyda," I say. "I need my day clothes. I must go to the kitchens."

Freyda hops to her feet and sets about laying out my garments. She is always very eager to please me — not because she is so fond of me, though I think she is — but because she does not wish to be sent back to her family where her lot would be to labour in the fields from dawn till dusk.

From previous experience, I know that my father will neglect to inform me of the impending visit even though I am a grown woman in my seventeenth year. Because there are no other women in residence, I am the female head of the household and expected to be at the king's side for all ceremonial occasions. Still, he will forget until the very last minute. But I have my own ways of finding out what is going on. One can learn much by visiting the kitchens. They are out behind the far end of the great hall and accessible only by a narrow, covered passageway that can be shut off from the hall in case of fire.

When I finally make my way there, a clattery bustle greets me. Warm and comforting smells hover in the air from the ever-present fire cauldrons in which bubble all manner of garden vegetables and scraps of meat. One of the two fat chief cooks is hollering at the kitchen boys to bring in some of the pig and the deer hanging in the smokehouse and to kill and pluck six of the yard chickens. The other sends one of the boys scurrying to the kitchen garden to gather herbs. Another boy is dispatched to the orchard to bring in apples and plums. Yet another is sent off to the fens to catch some eels.

A person of some import, indeed, I think to myself. Our usual fare of pottage, stew or broth, and hard bread will not suffice. But who can it be? I want to know.

When she has finished hurling orders about, Berga, the head chief cook, notices me standing just inside the door and bobs her head slightly in my direction. We do not stand on much ceremony here as my duties often bring me to the kitchen. Because Berga has been with my family since before I was born, she is the closest thing to a familiar I have in this house. No one else knows this but, since my mother died, Berga often goes to my father's bed in the dead of night when all his men are unconscious from drink. I have seen this with my own eyes.

"Berga, tell me what is happening."

"Only that your father has ordered a feast for the midday meal. A feast, mind you, with only a few hours to prepare," she grumbles.

"Do you know who our guest is to be?"

"Of course not! Only that it is a noblewoman from the north."

A woman!

"Your father told me that much so we would prepare dishes as befitting her sex and station. As though we have time to cook and bake fancy things," she grumbles some more.

"Thank you, Berga. I will leave you to get on with your work," I say, taking the hint.

"You'd best do something about that scraggly heap of straw on your head before the feast," Berga calls after me. "You'll want to do your father proud."

I wander back toward my room. I am still ruminating over who our visitor could be but without any satisfactory result as I have so little information to consider.

I fetch my bone comb from my little chest and begin to attend to my hair. It is difficult work because so many of the teeth in my comb are broken. I decide to wait until Freyda returns from wherever she is and let her deal with it. I content myself with my studies for awhile but concentration is elusive. More than once, I peer out my window slit to look down the road for dust.

Since my mother died and my sisters have all gone to be nuns in Francia or wives in some other kingdom, a woman is a rare commodity around here. The only women I know are the servants and the villagers. Sometimes, Berga acts as though she is my mother. My beloved sister, Seaxburga, went away to Kent to marry King Earconberht six years ago when I was only eleven. Since then I have yearned and prayed and wept silently in my bed at night for God to give me the company of a woman with whom I could share my thoughts and secrets.

Has this visitor been sent by God to me his humble servant? If so, I vow never again to question his wisdom in the construction of the human foot.

At last, there is a clattering commotion in the village. As the noise draws nearer and I can see the cause of it, a twinge of dismay stings me. The entourage consists of an open wooden wagon pulled by one horse, a driver, and four horse guards, one of whom is this morning's messenger.

How grand can this visitor be? I ask myself, fighting back tears of disappointment.

She is hunched in the back of the wagon, but I can scarcely make her out as a great brown cloak is gathered round her against the dust raised by the horses. The hood covering her head leaves her face in shadow.

As the wagon rattles up to the hall, the massive wooden doors open as if by magic. In truth, two of father's strongest men are pulling on the wheel ropes to make the doors swing back. My father steps out, dressed now in his best tunic and cloak. My younger brother, Iurminus, never far from my father's side, follows in his wake. I realize suddenly that I must hurry to join them to be present for the greeting. Fortunately, my chamber is the first one on the right beside the great doors, so I don't have far to go.

As I pick my way over the cobblestones, father is assisting the woman from the wagon. I hadn't noticed at first, but there is another smaller person in the cart for father to help down. When they are both safely on their feet, father dismisses the driver and the guards to the stables. "And send someone to fetch the village wise woman to see to that man's arm," he calls after them. "It's so putrid he may lose it."

"King Anna," the older woman murmurs as she bends her knee to my father. "I am deeply grateful for your hospitality."

"A kinswoman is always welcome in the royal house of East Anglia," my father replies in his most gallant manner. "Come, meet my children."

Iurminus steps up and gives a suitably royal nod in our visitor's direction as he has been taught to do by me. I suddenly feel an unaccustomed shyness and hold back.

"This is my son, Iurminus, and my daughter, Etheldreda." Seeing my hesitation, father calls to me, "Come, Dreda, come meet your kinswoman."

I urge myself forward. Unsure whether I should curtsey to her as an older woman and our guest or she to me as a royal princess, I do nothing. My father frowns slightly at my unusual awkwardness.

"Dreda, this is Lady Hild who has travelled from very far in the north.[16] She is sister to your Aunt Hereswitha."[17]

Lady Hild steps forward. I have to lower my eyes to hers as she is a head shorter than I. She takes both my hands in hers and says, "God's greeting to you, my child." All my silly inhibitions fly away as quickly as they had come, and my heart warms. "And this is my travelling companion and helper, Gerda."

We all offer a slight nod of acknowledgment in Gerda's direction.

The lady turns to my father. "Where is my sister, my lord? I imagined her here to greet me. Does she not live in your household since the death of her husband?"

"Ahhhh," breathes my father in a long sigh. "You do not know then. Your sister has already left East Anglia and has travelled to Gaul to the kingdom of the Franks. She has sought the religious life in the monastery of Chelles near Paris.[18] You did not know?" he asks again seeming at a loss.

Lady Hild's face crumples at the news. She is devastated and confused.

"How did this happen? I wished to meet her and travel with her to the land of the Franks and enter the religious life together there. It was always our plan for after she was widowed."

"We did not know you were coming, my lady. A group of travellers passed through here a few months back on their way to Gaul. Your sister was distraught over Æthelric's death and quickly decided to join them for the safety of numbers. A few members of this same group passed by here on their way home and reported that she was safely with the nuns at Chelles."

"God be praised that she is safe," murmurs Lady Hild. "And what of her son?"

"Ealdwulf is a stalwart young fellow. He is in training with my men who guard the dyke at Exning."

"But what shall I do?" She shakes her head dejectedly. "It has been a wretchedly long journey, and I cannot travel on alone. My guardsmen have been loaned to me by King Oswiu but only for the journey thus far. They are to return to Bernicia where Oswiu needs every man to show strength to Oswine in Deira. The warmongering among them is constant. I was given safe passage through Deira in respect for my great-uncle Edwin of sainted memory and because I am a woman and, therefore, of little consequence to these warlords. The guardsmen will have to return to Bernicia by another route."

"I am sorry to greet you with this distressing news, Lady Hild," says father, shaking his head in dismay. "Let me escort you to a chamber where you may rest. You may stay with us as long as you wish." He casts a glance at me and continues, "I can see by my daughter's face that the prospect of your visit being lengthened is a happy one for her. Perhaps, at some future time, another caravan will come by and you can travel with them to Chelles. In the meantime, you are our honoured guest for as long as need be."

Chapter Two

When the bone horn signals the beginning of the feast, my father enters the great hall, I on one arm and Lady Hild on the other. Iurminus follows next. King Cenwalh of Wessex, who, due to exile, has been a guest in our hall for two years now,[19] follows behind him.

A small gasp escapes me as I notice how the hall has been transformed. The strong sweet scent rising from fresh rushes on the floor helps to cover up the nose-pinching, acrid stench of men's unwashed bodies. All thirty-six of the wall torches burn brightly against the ever-present gloom of the hall. My father's men, those of his household guard who eat in the hall every day, have been ordered to make some efforts to improve their appearance and to behave with civility. Perhaps that means that this feast might not end, as others usually do, with a good-natured, drunken brawl.

A huge deer haunch claims pride of place in the centre of the great board, surrounded by platters of pig, chicken, and eel. Bowls of plums, apples, walnuts, chestnuts, and almonds and platters of cheese fill out the table. Great goblets sit waiting to be brim-filled from the pitchers of mead sitting before my place at the table.

My eyes well up at the sight. It floods my mind with memories of those long ago times when my mother and my sisters were here. With my being the sole woman remaining in the hall, standards have lowered considerably. It crosses my mind to be vexed that my father doesn't think my day-to-day presence warrants the same attention to civility as does that of our female guest. But I strive to drive that unworthy thought from my mind because I want to fully enjoy this moment. After all, haven't I put on my deep blue gown of finest wool and my silver arm rings and my mother's amethyst and gold pendant for the occasion? And didn't I endure Freyda's attention with the comb? Truth to tell, I feel a little overdressed as our guest wears only a drab brown, floor-length, coarse wool shift bound at the waist with a carved, leather belt and a matching cape draped over her shoulders. I think, perhaps a bit uncharitably, that she looks every bit the nun she is hoping to become. Well, at any rate, she wouldn't be inflaming the passions of my father's louty and uncouth household troops.

"You look very fetching, my dear," remarks Hild. "Your gown matches your eyes."

I thank her and wonder how I should respond. "That is a very fine belt you are wearing," I manage to say. "The tooling is well done." It seems to me a meager compliment, but Lady Hild smiles and her rather ordinary face lights up like the sun.

On the long boards below the salt, at which the men sit on benches, are four large blackened cauldrons containing this day's pottage. The contents are meant to lessen the men's ravenous appetites before they are allowed access to the feast. No lord would dare to exclude his men from the best part of the feast, and after the head board diners have heaped their plates, all the dishes will be passed down to the men to treat their bellies.

I begin my duty as my mother's surrogate and pour mead, first, as is his right, into my father's goblet and then into King Cenwalh's cup. Suddenly, I am unsure as to whether Iurminus or our lady guest should be next. I opt to fill Lady Hild's cup first, followed by my brother's goblet. An approving smile from my father tells me I made the correct decision. Then I continue around the great board and pour until all the men's cups are brimming. There is an abundance of backslapping and good humour among the men tonight. They love a good feast. I return to my place at the headboard.

My father then presents Lady Hild with the gift of a small gold cup, and she accepts it graciously as she must. He begins to parade all around the great board and with suitable flourish bestows pieces of gold on each of his household guards and on King Cenwalh and Iurminus. The men thump the table in appreciation of his generosity.

Father carves huge slabs from the deer for himself, Cenwalh, and Iurminus and slightly daintier ones for Lady Hild and me. When all the platters have been passed, he silences the hall with his raised hand and invokes prayers of thanksgiving for this bountiful feast and for the safe arrival of our guest. Now that all the ceremony has been completed in the right and proper manner, we are free to attend to our food.

"And so, my lady, how was your journey from the north?" father inquires as he rests between great mouths full of food. "Uneventful, I should hope, though your man's festering arm tells me differently."

"Not entirely uneventful, my lord. For the most part, we kept to the Roman roads for safety, but there were several times when we were forced to travel on woodland paths to achieve the next main road. On one of these occasions, we were beset by outlaws."

"These are indeed dangerous times," my father remarks. "Since you have all arrived safely, I gather your guards were successful against them. But is it a good story?"

"Quite good, my lord."

"Then will you honour us after the feast and be this day's tale-teller?"

"Would the men heed me?"

"It would be a diversion I am certain. We tell our old tales over and over till we know them by heart. A fresh one might capture their attention."

"Are your men Christian, my lord?"

"Of course! You must know East Anglia is a Christian kingdom."[20]

"I do. But sometimes great lords such as yourself are forced to hire mercenaries from pagan lands to help keep the peace and balance the power."

"Not so far, praise our Lord," says my father, making the sign of the cross. "But if that vile demon Penda turns his eyes on us again, it may come to that." His voice chokes on the bile of hatred. "He is the scourge of all Christian kingdoms in the land. After ignobly butchering the sainted Sigeberht, unweaponed as he was, and our former king, Ecgric,[21] Penda and his marauding warriors have been consumed, as I'm sure you know, with your homeland in the north. So we have been left alone for the time being."

"Indeed I know what a bane upon this land is Penda. I ask about your warriors only because my story might have more appeal for Christian men. And so, I will be honoured to be your tale-teller this night."

We eat on in relative silence for a little while, it being hard to make polite conversation while the men shout and jest at each other. I am very, very full but treats such as we are enjoying do not come along every day, and I am determined to make the most of them. Apparently, so are the men, who have begun to sprawl on the floor to relieve their bursting bellies from the pressure of sitting on a bench. Though their ale has been curtailed, they have managed to consume enough to raise the level of the teasing and taunting of one another. This usually signals an impending brawl.

Seeing this, my father stands up and all noise ceases.

"My brothers, I have a most welcome surprise for you this night. Our guest, Lady Hild, has consented to be our tale-teller."

A muted groan escapes the sprawling bodies, and one bolder voice speaks up. "What kind of tale will this be then?" he shouts, the ale feeding his insolence. "Will we be learning how to stitch or will it be a poem about flowers and lovers?"

The others guffaw heartily at his nervy wit.

"Silence!" roars my father. "Not another sound out of any of you. Our guest deserves your respect, and I promise you her tale will be worthy."

He sits down as Lady Hild rises to her feet. I watch in admiration. Though they are my father's trusted household guards, these men are brutish warriors. Even though I live with them day in and day out, I would no more consider addressing them than I would taking up a sword against them. But Lady Hild's voice rings with clarity and confidence throughout the timbers of the hall.

"Warriors and Christian men, heed my tale and let your immortal souls be raised by it. I am Hild of Northumbria, great-niece of King Edwin of sainted memory who, in the year of our Lord 627, caused himself and his household and all his chief men and many others to be baptized by Paulinus into the Christian faith.[22] I was among the baptized that day and have henceforward attempted to live and practise the faith. During the time of his exile, King Edwin was given refuge by the great lord of East Anglia, King Rædwald, brother of Eni, father of your own liege lord, King Anna."

At the recitation of these names, famed and revered among them, the warriors raise their sword arms and roar their salute. Lady Hild nods in agreement and waits for the noise to abate. I am astounded by her knowledge of our history and ancestors. When it is quiet again, she continues.

"From the north, I have journeyed to this hall to seek the company of my sister, Hereswitha, wife of Æthelric, brother of King Anna, on a further journey to France to enter there the convent of Chelles. But I find, to my great distress, that I am too late. My sister has left East Anglia. Your gracious king has offered me refuge. I shall be a guest in this hall for some time."

The men are becoming restless and beginning to grumble among themselves. They had expected a tale of heroics but instead are hearing a woman's story. Lady Hild raises her voice above the rumbling.

"I tell you all this by way of introduction. My tale really begins in the murky forests of Elmet."

With this masterstroke, she recovers their attention. Warriors love their tales to be set in the black shadows of deep primordial forests where all manner of evil spirits are believed to dwell and to wreak deadly havoc on the lives of ordinary mortals.

"Aye, Lady," one of the men calls out. "The evil one and his demons be in the forests. They come out of the mists and rip out the hearts of travelers and devour them while they still beat."

My father rewards him for his interruption with an icy stare and a clenched fist in his direction.

Lady Hild replies, "I have heard galdorcræft[23] permeates the deep shades of the forest where no sunlight dares go and terrified travellers have heard galdorsangs. There are many stories of the old ones who practise the arts of enchantment and wizardry and call on the old gods to work their dark ways. For myself, I believe the old ways display ignorance of the true faith and that belief in our Lord and Saviour overcomes evil and ignorance. I am sorry if it disappoints you, but there are no other-worldly demons in my tale."

Hild pauses while the men grumble for a bit then starts again.

"For the most part, my four horse guards, my driver, my companion, and I in the wagon travelled the Roman roads for safety. But there were times where, of necessity, we were forced to travel through the ancient forest to join another main road. This is where my tale begins."

Curiosity forces their attention back to her.

"No sunlight pierced the thick canopy of the forest. The air was black as midnight though, in truth, it was morning. We rumbled along a rutted cart path, jostling each other as we were tossed from side to side in the wagon. My helmeted guards, clad in thick leather armour emblazoned with Oswiu's crest, rode two in front and two in back. Their eyes raked the forest for signs of danger. As we passed, the eerie screeches of disquieted animals and birds set our spines tingling."

"And then," she pauses, "without warning the whole air about us was ripped with ear-splitting shrieks and unholy screams as a pack of outlaws descended upon our small train."

Some of my father's men shift a bit and sit up to pay better attention. This is more like it. For these men who live out their lives within the strictest of kin codes, outlaws have a certain fascination. None would truly wish to be an outlaw and all would strike them down without a thought if they encountered them.[24]

Lady Hild continues.

"Four men, former lord's men by the look of their ragged leather chest armour, were the leaders of a filthy, scantily clad band of at least twenty cutthroat ruffians. They descended the wooded hillside howling and brandishing huge wooden cudgels and short thrusting knives. My guards were sorely outnumbered, but they valiantly drew their swords and slashed about them as brigand after brigand attacked. The outlaw leaders tried to unhorse my men, but two of their number went down immediately with bloody gaping wounds to their necks. The fighting was fierce and deadly, and the Stygian forest air was rent with the piercing screams of the wounded and the dying. Sick at the sight of it, my companion and I huddled under our cloaks in the wagon and sobbed out prayers to our merciful Saviour.

"At length, the thudding of metal on wood and bone ceased, the horses no longer screamed, and the only sound was human whimpering. I peered out cautiously from beneath my cloak. The stench of slaughter flooded over me as I looked at the carnage surrounding the wagon. The bandits had been no match for Oswiu's trained soldiers. Their leaders lay sprawled in their own blood, unseeing eyes gazing toward heaven. Fifteen or more bloodied bodies, some missing limbs and heads, were strewn about while five survivors cowered beneath the hooves of the soldiers' horses. One of my guards had taken a sword gash to his arm. One of the others was tying a leather thong above the wound to staunch the streaming blood."

My father's men whoop and drum their fists on the long boards to signal their satisfaction at the outcome. At length, my father raises his hand to silence them and nods to Lady Hild to continue.

"The captain of the guard, Ælfric by name, could barely contain his uninjured soldier's killing lust while he looked to see if we were unharmed."

"We are safe, praise be to God!" I assured him.

He nodded and gave the signal to his two good-armed men. "You may wish to avert your eyes, my lady," he warned.

"Stop!" I commanded.

The listeners' eyes pop, and their mouths gape in astonishment. What kind of woman would dare to interfere with a soldier intent on finishing off the enemy, especially outlaws?

"The two soldiers lowered their swords and wheeled to look to their captain for the order to slaughter the survivors."

"You cannot execute these people," I said. "One is a mere child."

"But, my lady," Ælfric protested, "they will only go into the woods to find the rest of their tribe and be back at us in a few hours."

"You cannot just kill them," I stated. "It is against God's laws."

Groans of disgust escape my father's men. Though they are all professed Christians, they seldom let that fact stand in the way of a righteous killing spree.

"Why can we not kill them?" Ælfric demanded angrily. "We killed their fellows."

"That was in defense of us, for which I am most grateful. But these few ragtag survivors pose no threat to us now. It would be a crime against God to kill them. Are you not a Christian, sir?"

"Yes"

"And your men?"

"We were all baptized as children by Paulinus at York[25] when the great King Edwin ordered it."

"I, too, was baptized that same blessed Eastertide in the year of our Lord 627 in the church of St. Peter the Apostle at York. Well then, you must do more than profess your belief. You must live within God's laws," I chided him. "You would do well to look to your men's souls as well as your own before you slaughter these helpless creatures."

"Ælfric was torn between his duty to his God and his obligation to his men. And he did not like my speaking to him in this way."

A rumble arises among the listeners. Clearly, they side with Ælfric.

"Life is cheap to these people," argued Ælfric. "They don't care if they live or die. Their lives are harsh and meaningless. Wouldn't it be a boon to them to dispatch them to their heavenly father?"

"Do you know for certain that heaven receives the unshriven souls of those killed while committing a crime? If we expect to receive mercy from our all-loving and all-powerful God, then we must be willing to show mercy to others while we live. Let them go in peace, Ælfric. It is my wish."

"But my soldiers," Ælfric grumbled. "If they attack again, we run the risk of one of us being killed."

"Did you lose any today?"

"No," Ælfric admitted. "But look at Thorag's arm!"

"He will mend. I must insist that you release the captives back into the forest. The woods are full of outlaws. If we are attacked again, it would probably be a different band entirely. We cannot afford to sit here arguing all day. We must get to the Roman road and to shelter before nightfall."

"Ælfric clearly resented my ordering him about, not wanting his men to smell weakness in their leader who did the bidding of a mere woman, but at last, he wheeled his horse and called off his men. The cowering ruffians, sensing that they were to be inexplicably spared, melted into the forest in an instant. All except the boy, who scrambled between the legs of the guards' horses and hoisted himself up on the wagon frame. After planting a tender kiss on my hand, he too was gone."

"Let us proceed, Ælfric," I said. "We will not be attacked by this particular outlaw band again."

"The two unwounded guardsmen dismounted and dragged the bloody and broken corpses off to the side of the path. We all agreed to take a ship as soon as one could be found and continue our journey by sea. Here ends my tale."

The listeners bang the boards again to signal that it had, indeed, been a tale worth the telling. As Lady Hild sits down, my father rises to his feet.

"We will let the women retire," he declares. "Two of you fellows go out to the stables and escort the heroic Ælfric, who in the end saw his Christian duty, and his men into the hall. We will toast their bravery and finish off what mead may remain." He turns to his guest. "Our thanks, Lady Hild, for a fine tale."

We are being dismissed so the men can begin carousing. I loathe this part of the feast. During these noisy revels that go on into the night, there is little sleep to be found in our beds until they all fall into a drunken stupor. I wonder again for the hundredth time why men take such pleasure in being brutish and crude and smelly.

Chapter Three

The next morning, after terce[26] prayers and breaking the fast, Lady Hild and I set out on foot to walk round the village. We are accompanied by a kitchen boy who lugs a wooden cart groaning with packages of leftover feast food wrapped in scraps of sacking.

"Your father is generous to his people," Hild remarks.

"Yes, he knows well the obligations of kingship," I reply.[27] "He must uphold the laws of the land and maintain the security of his serfs and slaves. He feels responsibility for their well-being in other ways as well. He is fond of saying that a healthy, well-fed, and grateful man will be a superior subject to a downtrodden, ravenous, and embittered man."

"Does he say the same for the women?" Hild asks.

"Of course not. Men only speak of men when they are talking in generalities. It is up to the husbands and fathers to see to their own women."

The rattling of the cart on the rutted village lanes brings the women, small children, and baying hounds to the doorways of their wattle and daub huts.[28] Word would have spread of yesterday's feast, and they are expecting us. Wafts of smoke from the cooking fire in the centre of the dirt floor in each hut escape through the doorways as we pass. From the thatched roofs, startled chickens scuttle and cluck at us.

I like this ritual of passing out leftover feast food to the villagers. They smile and nod their thanks and say things like, "God bless you, child" or "Go with God" or "God bless your father." I like that I feel, in a small way, that I am doing God's work.

It warms me.

At first, the village women look askance at Lady Hild. We all learn early to be wary of strangers no matter their gender or station. But, when they learn she is a woman of God, they welcome her.

When we have distributed all the food, I tell the kitchen boy to return the wagon to the stable and go to Berga, where he will be needed for the midday meal. Lady Hild and I take a more leisurely route back to the hall, sitting on a stone bench alongside the river and enjoying the cooler, cleaner air there.

"I was baptized in a stream like this," I remark.

"Where was that now?" Lady Hild inquires.

"Our family lived at Exning then. Sigebert was king and lived here at Rendlesham. My father was his general. He and his men defended the dykes from invasion, especially from the Mercians."[29]

"Who performed the baptism?"

"Bishop Felix. He came one day and our whole family and some of the servants and soldiers gathered at the stream where we were all baptized together."

"How did you feel about it?"

"I was merely a child of seven, so I didn't really understand what was happening, but I remember thinking that it was a good thing. After we came to Rendlesham, I went to the Bishop's school for many years. It was there that I was educated in Roman Christianity and Latin and was taught needlework and manuscript illumination."

"By Bishop Felix?"

"King Sigebert founded the school to teach boys, and Felix was the head teacher, but some royal and noble girls were allowed to study there under pressure from my father. We taught each other needlework, and the scribes taught us illumination. Bishop Felix himself educated me in the Christian way and was my Latin tutor. My father probably ordered him to do this. But he didn't seem to mind that I was a girl."[30]

"Was he a man that you liked?" Lady Hild asks.

"I suppose I did but, like all men, his body and his clothing were smelly, so I didn't like to stand too close to him. At least he spoke of things of the spirit and the Greek and Roman ways of thinking about the world, unlike my father's men who just think about warfare and killing."

"Do you no longer go to the school?"

"No," I reply, sadly. "Bishop Felix ascended into the heavenly kingdom in the spring of this year just before you came. I shall miss his teachings, but father says I am well enough educated now."[31]

"When did you come to Rendlesham?" Lady Hild asks.

"When Penda made my father king under him."

"How many winters had you had at that time?"

"Ten. The whole village was burned to the ground. Penda had slaughtered every single soul. My Uncle Egric's head was impaled upon a pike in front of the still smoldering great hall, and all about us were the charred bodies of women, children, and old men."[32]

Though I state the details flatly without emotion, the foulness and terror of the horrific scene we had come upon at Rendlesham engulfs me again as fresh as the day it happened. The memory of the stench still pinches my nose, and I begin to weep. Lady Hild sits calmly beside me and takes my hand until the sobbing subsides.

"That is a tormenting memory for a young girl to carry all these years," she says quietly and I feel strangely comforted.

"You said at the feast that you were baptized with King Edwin's family," I say to her, changing the subject.

"Yes, that's true, child. I am a member of the family of King Edwin of sainted memory."

"Why do you say 'of sainted memory' each time you say his name?"

"Because he truly was a saintly man and king. He brought peace to all of Britain wherever his authority extended. It was said that in his time as king, a mother could walk with her newborn babe from one sea to the other with no fear of harm coming to either of them. He took such care of his people that he caused stakes with brass cups hanging from them to be erected near clear springs by the highways so that travellers would never have cause to thirst in his land.[33] It was the greatest pride of my father, Hereric, to be King Edwin's nephew.

"During the wars between Bernicia and Deira in Northumbria, Edwin was exiled as was my father. Perhaps you know this story. Edwin sought refuge here in East

Anglia at the court of Rædwald. The king of Northumbria, Æthelfrith, demanded that Rædwald surrender Edwin or kill him. Instead, Rædwald raised a great army and defeated the Northumbrians at the River Idle and killed Æthelfrith. He put Edwin on the throne. This all happened in the year of our Lord 616, when I was a child of two years."

"And what of your father?"

"He was murdered in Elmet, the very same land where the outlaws fell on us on our journey here. He was seeking sanctuary there."

"I'm sorry."

"It was a long time ago, child, and I didn't know him as my older sister did. My mother, Breguswith, searched and searched for him until she learned he was dead. Have you not heard all of this from your Aunt Hereswitha?"

"I hardly knew her. We did not sit and talk like this. She was much older and when we were at feasts with family, she was more interested in two of my older sisters who were going to monasteries in France. I think she wanted to do that herself long before my uncle's death."

"I agree. She was not suited to secular life."

"What has your life been until now," I ask.

"I do not talk about my life before now," Lady Hild replies in a tone that tells me there is no point in asking any further. "It is of no importance to me," she continues. "When I began instruction for the church under my beloved mentor, Aidan, Bishop of Lindisfarne, a few years ago, that is when my life began."[34]

"Does that mean your studies into the faith have taken you along the Celtic way?" I ask.

"Yes," she replies.

"Then do you believe that is the true way to heaven?" I ask, a bit alarmed. "Bishop Felix was very clear that the Roman way is the only true way to Christ."

"I think, child, that there is more than one true way to heaven just as there is more than one way for me to return to Northumbria. If a soul believes in one of the true ways, that soul will be received into heaven with just as much joy as a soul who has pursued another true way."

"Felix believed the Roman way is the only true way," I repeat stubbornly.

"Well, I am sorry to say this about a bishop of the church, but I believe that teaching is nonsense."

A small gasp inadvertently escapes me, and I hastily make the sign of the cross.

"If you let yourself think about it," Lady Hild goes on, ignoring my outburst, "you will realize that there cannot be only one path to heaven. One would have to entirely discredit the beliefs and teachings of the Irish fathers, Patrick[35] and Columba.[36] It is only reasonable to accept that there will be some differences in the rituals and the doctrines. Have you not thought this way before?"

"Bishop Felix likes to tell me what I should think, but I do not always obey."

"You are free to think what you want, child. No one controls your thoughts. You may not have been allowed to express such an idea though. You have learned your lessons well at Bishop Felix's school, but you have not yet learned how to think for yourself. I see that I must take this aspect of your education on myself. It is the most important skill you will acquire, and it will make all the difference to your future life."

"I already know what my future life will be," I reply, sadly. "Father will marry me to someone who has an army strong enough to help him defend our kingdom from invaders, just as he did with my sister, Seaxburga."

"Tell me again where she is."

"In the south, in Kent. Five years ago, my father made an alliance for her to marry King Earconberht so both the kingdoms would be stronger when Penda comes again, which he will. Now that wicked devil is consumed with waging war in your homeland, but he will tire of that and come here again because we are easier prey. I know this because I listened to father and his Witan talking. His council men do not think East Anglia is strong enough even with the Kentish alliance, so they are urging my father to make another alliance through a marriage for me."

"What do you think about that?"

"I do not want it. I do not like men, and I cannot imagine lying with one. They are big and noisy and smelly. They do not want educated women. They only want women who will give them sons and manage the household servants and slaves."

"What do you want then?"

"I want to go to Francia with you. My other sisters were allowed to go there to enter the religious life. I should be able to as well."

"Are you certain that is what you desire? You must give up everything for that life."

"What would I be giving up?" I ask. "I would still be able to study and eat and pray and go to mass, and I could do it all without listening to my father's men belching and farting and cursing all day."

Lady Hild doubles over with laughter.

"A compelling argument, I admit," she finally manages to say. "Shall I speak to your father?"

"If you wish, but it will do no good. Even a king must be guided by his councillors, and they have already begun negotiations for a husband for me."

"With whom?"

"I do not know nor will I until it has all been arranged."

"You are very fair of face, child. I am sure prospective husbands will be standing in line."

"There may be some who are willing, but it will be the one who is best able to help defend the kingdom who will be chosen." Rising to leave, I say, "We must return to the hall for the midday meal. Father will be wondering where we are."

"Nevertheless, I intend to approach your father and learn for myself where he stands on this issue. I have been known to be quite persuasive when I believe in my cause. Do not despair yet, my child."

Chapter Four

Because we had given all the leftover feast food to the villagers, that day at the boards we eat pottage and slabs of hard bread, which we soften by dipping it in the thick soup. My father announces there will be a hunt on the morrow. There is much hooting and backslapping among the men who relish a hunt almost as much as a skirmish. Father says they need to replenish the stores for they will soon be riding out for many days to check the border defenses and meet with the ealdormen.[37]

I retire early that evening for I know from experience that I will be awakened before dawn when the hunting party assembles on the cobbled courtyard outside the great hall.

Twenty snorting steeds squirt puffs of white mist from their nostrils and paw the cobbles impatiently in the sharp pre-dawn air. Their riders hurl good-natured boasts at each other over who will have the best kill. When father arrives sitting tall and straight on his charger, they raise their spears and holler a salute. Iurminus rides slightly behind astride his beloved palfrey chosen today over his warhorse for its speed and agility in the hunt. King Cenwalh follows him. No man wears cumbersome armour or carries war shields this day in order to be lighter and faster in pursuit of their prey.

Father raises his hand, and the men fall silent. As anxious as the rest to begin the hunt, he briefly acknowledges Lauds,[38] though it is not yet six, by reciting the first two verses of the fifty-first Psalm. He falls silent, and the men say to themselves whatever private things are in their hearts.

Then thrice bellows the bone horn, and the hunting party, father at the head, begins the slow trot through Rendlesham's street. At the bleating of the horn, doors fly open, and villagers step over their thresholds, raising their arms in a closed-fisted salute and shouting their hopes for a prosperous hunt.

When they have disappeared into the morning mist, Lady Hild and I go to the chapel to say a proper Lauds. After the psalms, in private prayer, I speak to God about what Lady Hild had said the day before. I tell him that she desires to help me go into the church. Surely he would want that, wouldn't he? I ask for a sign of hope for her success. My mind wanders away from my prayers, and I begin to think about father. He seems to like Hild, even respect her, so he might listen. If she were not so steadfastly bound for the church, I think he might even consider taking her to be his wife, and then I would have a mother again. But he would have to overthrow the Witan's decision, and he would never do that. He would say a king must be guided by the wisdom of his councilors, just as a daughter must heed the wisdom of her father. No, unless God intervenes in some mysterious way, there is no hope for me. I pray some more but the futility of it all washes over me. Unbidden tears trickle down my cheeks and plink on the cold stone slab on which I kneel.

Some hours later, the bone horn bleats again to signal the return of the huntsmen. They clatter up to the courtyard with an air of high excitement, and I can see instantly through my window slit that they have been successful. Father's face is flushed with the consumption of much victory ale. The freshly bloodied antlers of a twelve point stag are tied round his head with leather thongs. The backs of the packhorses sag under the heavy carcasses of deer, boar, and loads of smaller animals and birds, all bleeding from spear wounds.

Forming a circle, the party trots slowly round the yard showing off their good fortune to the unlucky men who had drawn the unmarked stones the previous night. They stayed home to guard the hall and the women and children. Though they had been deprived of the pleasure of the hunt, they clap and stamp their feet in good-natured salute to the hunters, knowing that they too will share in the bounty when it arrives at the boards.

The skinners and butchers appear in their leather aprons stained with old blood and lead the packhorses and their loads away. The hides will be sent to the tanners, the meat will be hung, and the offal fed to the hounds, who are already slinking about and barking at the hoofs of the packhorses. The chandler will use the stinking tallow to make candles, and the bones will be bleached and given to the carvers. Perhaps I will receive a new comb. Even the hoofs will be boiled down for glue. When the after-hunt ceremony is over, the hunters all retire to the great room in the hall to continue their boasting and carousing.

I hope they will be weary enough to fall asleep when the drink takes over their wits.

A few days later, Lady Hild comes to my chamber to collect me as she has made an appointed time to petition my father.

"I don't think I should be present," I say, hanging back.

"Of course, you must," she insists. "You must make your father say to your face whatever his decision is."

I comply grudgingly. I believe she is trying to help me, but I know my situation is hopeless. There has been no sign from God. Indeed, he has been inexplicably silent on the subject.

Father is sitting in the carved wooden king's chair at the head of the great hall, the stag's antlers now bound by the leather thongs to either side of the back posts. Thankfully, he has cleared the men from the room while he hears our petition. A fire crackles and spits in the grate. Because this is a formal petition he motions Lady Hild to come forward and kiss his ring in obeisance before waving to the chairs that have been placed before him. He bids me kiss his cheek. When we are both settled, he nods in Lady Hild's direction signalling that she can begin.

"Lord King Anna," she opens, in her most deferential manner, "since I have been a guest in your hall, your hospitality has been both generous and respectful. I believe you to be a good Christian man who would desire to give his daughter the happy, fulfilled life she deserves and one that you have already bestowed on some of her older sisters. In our time together, Princess Etheldreda and I have talked at length about her future. She wishes nothing more than to enter religious life in one of the convents of the Frank's land. My petition this day asks if there is any impediment to her accompanying me over the channel and taking her vows?"

For fully a minute, my father sits in dark silence, his left elbow resting on the chair arm and his forefinger and thumb playing with his lip. I quiver a little, wondering if he will bellow at such boldness from a guest in his hall, and a female guest at that. When he does speak, his voice is firm but tinged with the sorrow of a powerful man who has not the power to do as he wills.

"Lady Hild," he begins, "I am aware that my beloved daughter wishes to enter religious life and, by rights, she should be able to follow in the steps of her sisters, but it is beyond my power to grant her wish. The Witan has agreed that she must have a husband who has the strength of an army under his command to help us protect our lands. We are not now strong enough within ourselves to do this. When Penda tires of scourging the north, he will turn his sights towards us again. It is my bitter burden to know that I am king in East Anglia only because Penda of Mercia allows me to be. Though I am a true Wuffinga[39] and the rightful ruler of this kingdom, Penda defeated our armies and killed our kings several years ago. By right of conquest he rules this country. He set me on this chair because it suited him to do so. When he decides to come into East Anglia again, we must be ready to defend ourselves.

"As a king, I agree with the Witan's decision that we must have another alliance such as the one with Eorconberht of Kent to whom we married Dreda's sister, Seaxburga. Penda is a mighty warrior driven by the devil's bloodlust, and we will need all the support we can muster to defend against him. But, as a father, it is a great sorrow to me to deny my daughter her desire. God has granted us this life above the slaves and the serfs and the farmers and the craftsman, but there are obligations and responsibilities attached to it that we cannot ignore. Dreda has enjoyed a life of education and privilege thus far. Now has come the time for her to accept her responsibilities to her people and her king.

"I must, therefore, deny your petition. We will not speak of this again."

Returning to my chamber, I sit on my little stool staring bleakly through the window slit. Lady Hild has come with me. She is pacing up and down the smooth stone floor, muttering under her breath. She has lost, and she is unhappy about it. I had known this would be the outcome and, therefore, am not as disappointed as she, but I feel oppressed by the burden of my duty as a royal princess of the Wuffingas.

After a time, she stops pacing and kneels down beside me. She takes my cold hand in hers and says, "Sometimes this hard world demands more of us than is fair, my child, but I am certain that God has a plan for you. We must be patient and pray that, in time, all will be revealed. I believe your desire for the religious life will be fulfilled but not now. I fear you must abide in the secular world awhile yet."

"Oh, Lady Hild," I cry, suddenly angry, "why is it that God allows those men to make a decision that keeps me from his work?"

"God's ways are not always known to us, child. You must know this and you must accept the mystery of it."

"But I feel that I am not a real person, just a chattel that has not the ability to exercise a will of its own. What is the good of being a royal princess if I am treated as a cow in the field that has no say in its life?"

"You will become stronger. You will find a way to be your own person. I see the seeds of that already in you. You must be content to give those seeds time to sprout and bloom. It will happen, I assure you. I, myself, have only now answered the call to enter into religious life at the age of thirty-three, the same age as our dear Saviour when he died on the cross for us, and almost twice your years. You must find a way to be patient. Meanwhile, I will pray for you every day. You must remember that every single day a prayer for your strength is winging its way to the Heavenly Father. You will gradually feel your resolve harden, and it will take you places you do not now think possible."

Chapter Five

Life at the hall continues as before. Father and his retainers and Iurminus set out for the borders, leaving a skeleton force under Wessex to guard the hall. Lady Hild and I continue our talks. Like a sponge, I soak up her knowledge and understanding of this wondrous new religion we have given our hearts to. I feel closer to her than any other person. I think she feels the same toward me.

One day during one of our talks, she tells me, "Child, it is not necessary to address me as Lady Hild when we are just talking between us. I hope we have become very good friends, so I would like to call you Dreda, as your family does, and you may call me Hild, as my family does. How do you feel about this?"

Joy washes over me at this singular honour.

"I would like that very much. Thank you, Hild," I say, the name by itself falling a little strangely from my tongue.

"You are welcome, Dreda," she replies, smiling. "Now there is no distance between us."

The harvest is over and the crops are all safe in the barns and sheds. The farmers now work alongside the woodsmen to bring in enough wood for all in the village and hall to be warm through the winter.

Father and his men return, and the relative peace of the hall is shattered once again by their hearty boorishness. I notice that Iurminus is losing his smooth boyish skin and trying very hard to be one of the men. A little stubble of beard, fair in colour like our hair, is beginning to appear. I sense that father's attitude toward me has changed in some significant way. He seems to treat me less as a child and more as the woman I have been in my own mind for some time. I wonder vaguely what this means.

The days become frostier. Hild, who fears all forests after her encounter with the outlaws, enlists Wessex and a few of the household men to be our guardsmen while we gather evergreen boughs and heaping cart loads of holly and mistletoe from the forest to festoon the hall for Christmastide. Three days before Christ's Mass Day, the woodsmen haul in the great Yule log on a sledge drawn by two snorting plough horses. They plod right into the hall and up to the hearth where the woodsmen roll the log till one end is in the fire. As the days go on, and the end of the log burns down, it will be pushed further and further into the fire pit. It will last until we have finished celebrating the Holy season of Christ's birth.

For the moment, all is well in the kingdom, and father is in a magnanimous mood. At the boards, he announces a three-day Yule holiday during which there will be contests of horsemanship along with axe and spear throwing competitions for the men and games of leap frog and blind man's bluff for the children. At the end of the festivities, the villagers will be invited to the hall for a great feast to welcome the new calendar year and the lengthening of the day's light. I decide to stay as far away as possible from the kitchens over the coming days because Berga will be in high flourish, hurling orders about and boxing the ears of the kitchen boys if they slack even a little.

Before we know it, modraniht[40] arrives, and the festivities begin. I preside over the Yule celebrations and feasting not so much as the mascot of the hall but as an adult partner. I can not be sure whether the change is in father or in me, but either way I am gratified by my newfound sense of self.

Hild and I sit vigil in the chapel during the Night of the Mothers. During the long night, we pray to the mother of Christ to care for all mothers everywhere the Christian faith is known and in other parts of the world where the inhabitants have not yet learned of the wondrous true God. Father and Iurminus and Cenwalh come in from time to time to kneel with us on the cold stone floor.

Early in the morning of Christ's Mass Day, Hild and I come to the great hall to find that the huge fir tree has been brought in overnight and stands like a sentinel in the centre of the hall. After a few hours of blessed sleep, we will return and festoon the tree with ropes of bright-berried holly and mistletoe. We will hang fruit from the boughs and set the tapers so they will be ready to light for the feast.

After we have celebrated the mass, Father sits in his great throne chair and hears petitions from a few of the villagers who are hoping to take advantage of the Christ's Mass Day tradition of offering pardons for minor infractions. Ladders have been brought in, and two of the kitchen boys have been spared their duties for a short time so that they can scramble up the ladders and hang the fruit and attach the beeswax tapers, used only for very special occasions, to the higher boughs. Hild, Iurminus, and I stay safely on the ground and festoon the lower branches. Soon all is ready for the feast.

Once again the bone horn sounds, and we all parade in to the headboard, which is groaning under the weight of a whole roasted boar, brown and dripping with luscious juices and fat. I am wearing a beautiful new emerald green gown of a wondrous soft material that father has given me as a Yuletide gift. I wear a string of emeralds about my neck and several gold bands on my arms. Hild wears a flowing white gown of very fine wool. I recognize it as belonging to my mother and reckon that father has loaned it to her for a Yule gift. It looks well on her short, slim frame. I notice, too, that Iurminus is displaying a very fine new sword at his side, also a Yule gift from father. Cenwalh and my father are each garbed in their best robes. Altogether we make a very fine presentation at the royal headboard. Even the household men appear to have had a scrub and dragged out clean tunics for the occasion.

Spirits are high for this best of all days. It is time for the tapers on the tree to be lit. The hall will be magical when they are glowing. We all sit in awed silence as the kitchen boys raise the ladders again and, beginning at the top, light the tapers. Gradually, the dimness of the great room, till now lit only by firelight, begins to fade and is replaced by the holy glow of a hundred tapers sending their lovely light to God. The beauty of it brings unbidden tears of joy trickling down my cheeks.

The boys take their places beside four large buckets of water that have been placed near the tree. Their job is to keep their eyes pinned on the tree for the very first sign of smoke or fire. If they waver for a moment in this responsibility, they will be sent away from their kitchen positions and returned to their families where they will be put to back breaking work in the fields.

While I fill the mead cups, father goes from man to man and hands out his gifts of gold and silver and precious stones. When he returns to the royal board, he raises his arms for silence and intones a prayer of gratitude for the peace we are experiencing in our kingdom and of thanksgiving for the bountiful harvest and the feast before us. As soon as he is finished, toasting with mead cups, laughter and other sounds of merriment ring through the hall. The Christ's Mass Day festivities are well on their way for another year.

I am sprawled out on my cot vowing never to eat another morsel as long as I live. My normally flat belly is plumped up by my excesses at the table over the last several days. I think about the holidays and smile at the memories.

The games were a great success with the champion receiving a new set of leather armour as his prize. Each of the children received a coin from the hand of the king for their participation. The walls of the great hall were bursting when all the village families and the families of my father's house guards gathered to usher in the new year and the beginning of the days of longer light. There was no room for ceremony, so the food was laid out on the headboard and everyone just helped themselves. After all had received a coin from the king and returned to their homes, the hall was left in a mess of catastrophic proportions. All manner of vermin scurried around feasting on dropped morsels of food and discarded bones. The floor slates were besmeared with grease and slopped drink, and the rushes were filthy and broken. It is a good thing that the men have gone home with their families for a few days so the household servants will have time to scour the hall before they return.

As I lie here with bursting belly and the door to my chamber firmly bolted, I am hoping that the rats and mice and other vermin have eaten their fill and have taken themselves back to their nests to sleep off their holiday excesses.

With the Yule season over and winter settling in properly, the air slices at our bones like knives. Hild and I are forced to shorten our daily walkabouts. We pass our days saying the offices in the chapel and, in between psalms and prayers, we sew and talk before a warming fire in my chamber. The guest chambers do not have a grate. I always wondered if that is to discourage lengthy stays. If so, it doesn't appear to be a successful strategy as Hild has now been in residence with us for several months, and Wessex has been here for more than two years.

Talk of Hild's leaving in the spring has crept into our conversations, and it makes my stomach churn to think of her not being here. She has become the mother and sister I have craved for so long, and I have become firmly attached to her. I admire her wisdom, I covet her grace, and I exuberantly assimilate her understanding of our faith into my heart and mind.

And then, one day, the world that I have created for myself is cleft in two as surely as though a broad axe had fallen on it.

Chapter Six

Spring has arrived at last, and with it, the new year in the fields and forests.[41] The meadows are bursting with colour, and the tree branches sag under the weight of their blossoms. Birds dart everywhere, singing and chirping and building their nests. Lambing and calving and foaling have begun, and the fields are alive with the joyful gamboling of these innocent new lives.

Then the messenger comes.

I am only passing curious about his business until he asks for Lady Hild. Then my interest is excruciating. I can scarcely keep myself in my chamber though I know I should.

He stays only long enough to hand a small packet to Hild and to take some nourishment in the kitchens. Then he is off again.

The midday meal has been over for a while, and the hall is relatively quiet. The king's men have been dispatched to their own lands for a few days to supervise the tilling and seeding of their fields, to count the livestock, record the newborns, and to inspect the health of their slaves and servants. They will also visit with their wives and children if they have any.

I sit on the stool by the window slit sewing my tiny, perfect embroidery stitches onto a border around the hem of a fine new robe father has bought for me from some passing peddlers. I force my hand to be steady while my nerves are jangling with suspense. Because the light is beginning to fade, I know I will have to stop soon.

At last, there is a quiet knocking at my chamber door.

"Enter," I call out, forcing myself to sound calm.

Hild steps into the room and closes the door after her. Her face is radiant. The tired lines around her eyes and mouth seem to have disappeared. She is smiling, and her clear blue eyes sparkle with light.

"My child," she cries, stepping toward me, "you will not believe my news! I can scarcely take it in myself."

I know then that all the catastrophic notions my mind has conjured about the import of the message are going to come true. Something significant has happened, and I am not going to like it.

Anxious to know but not wanting to hear, I dismiss Freyda from the chamber before asking, "What is it?"

"Bishop Aidan, my mentor and the teacher to whom I owe all my understanding of our faith, has written pleading with me to return to my homeland. He desires me to begin a monastery there on lands he will provide along the River Wear. It is to be a double house on the French model,[42] and I am to be the abbess!"

My heart drops. The joy this news instills in her is manifest.

"I have spent these last hours in the chapel praying and waiting for God to tell me what to do." Her words burble over each other. "Then I realized he has already given me my answer through Aidan's missive. Instead of travelling to France, God wants me to go home and continue his work there. Imagine! It has been my long-held dream to be an abbess and to be able to guide the lives of young women in the faith."

Apparently, at that moment, she notices my lack of enthusiasm for the plan as she abruptly stops talking. After a deep breath, she continues.

"Oh, my dear, I am sorry. I have been going on so without regard for your feelings. How callous of me! I am so sorry. I realize this news changes everything but I have only been thinking about myself."

My devastation makes me cruel.

"It is all right, Hild," I reply coldly. "Please do not concern yourself with me. You have been offered a shining new life, and I have my duty. It is the way of things."

"If your father would make it possible, I would take you with me. You must know this."

"Yes," I reply distantly. "I have always known this day would come. I suppose I should rejoice that you are staying on this side of the channel and not scuttling off to Francia after all."

"Oh, Dreda," she says, her joyful spirits flattened by my churlishness. "Please do not be unkind. You must celebrate with me in this. It is what God wants for me. It will be important work, meaningful work for the kingdom of God."

Who can argue with that?

"I'm sorry," I say, feeling ashamed of my words. "I have only been thinking of my own miserable self, as well. It is just that I have not yet achieved eighteen years, and I have lost all the women I have ever loved. My mother died, my older sisters went to France, and Seaxburga has gone to Kent, and now you are going home to the north. And I will be left again in a house full of raucous men, who only think about hunting and carousing. Who will I talk to?"

"You will soon have a household of your own to manage and children to bring love into your life. You will be happy. In the meantime, you must talk to God."

"My duty requires me to marry for a military and political alliance, but it does not require me to submit to my husband. And I have decided that I will not, ever. I will remain a virgin throughout my life, so that I will be a suitable bride for Christ when my time comes."

"I do not think that virginity is a requirement for the religious life. Many wives have brought forth children and then entered a French convent as widows. My sister, Hereswitha, is an example."

"Nevertheless, I have made a covenant with God, and I will not break it."

"And when did you make this covenant?"

"Some weeks ago."

"Yet you did not tell me of it."

"I told no one. It is between me and God," I say, then add, "well I suppose it is now between me and God and you."

"Will you not tell your father?"

"It is not his concern," I say, stubbornly.

"It may well be his concern when he forges a marriage alliance for you. Your prospective husband may not be so willing if he knows you have pledged yourself to the Almighty."

"That is a dilemma, I see. I have no wish to weaken the kingdom by my intransigence. Perhaps I will ask father to find me an old husband who is beyond carnal desires and only wishes companionship."

"Is there such a man?"

"I know not but I will think on it," I say, dismissing the subject. "When will you go?" I ask sadly, realizing that I must summon up some measure of grace and accept this turn of events with at least a small show of composure.

"Bishop Aidan has told me in his missive that a ship returning to the north will stop along the coastline in May. They will send a messenger to Rendlesham for my response. If it is no, they will go on without me. If yes, I must be prepared to return immediately with the messenger. I am sorry for my companion, Gerda. She is not a good sailor. The prospect of a lengthy sea voyage will upset her. She has been dreading the channel crossing ever since our shorter voyage here. She was deathly ill the whole time, poor thing."

"Perhaps she will stay and work in our household. Freyda would like that as they seem to have become friends."

"I doubt she will do that," replies Hild. "She is as dedicated to God as you are and wants only to become a nun. Her distress at the sea voyage will be offset by her joy at entering a monastery in her home kingdom instead of a foreign land."

In this moment, I wonder how it is that I, a princess, can envy a servant girl.

"Then it is settled. You are really leaving?"

"Oh, yes, my child, I must. It is my destiny that was foretold in a dream to my mother. When my father was in exile, my mother had a dream in which she was searching everywhere for him. At last, she looked in the folds of her garment where she found a precious jewel. While she looked on it, it cast such a light as spread itself throughout all Britain. Later, the dream was interpreted that I am the jewel, and I must do everything in my power to spread the light of God throughout the land."[43]

"Then I must take this next month to prepare myself for your departure," I say, with reluctant resignation. "Will we still walk along the river and talk as we have?"

"Of course we will. Since Gerda and I brought so few possessions with us, it will take very little time for us to be ready. I must arrange an appointed time to tell your father. The news may not distress him overmuch. I have noticed his manner toward me has cooled somewhat after our petition."

"He is probably just absorbed with affairs of the kingdom. Sometimes, he barely speaks to me for days on end."

"Perhaps that is it," replies Hild, though she sounds unconvinced.

Chapter Seven

The days of April fly by at an alarming rate drawing ever closer to the time when I will say farewell to my beloved friend. Deep inside me I know she is charting the right course for herself, but I wonder sadly if I will ever see or hear of her again.

Hild has delivered the news of her departure to my father. She tells me he seemed relieved though he tried to hide it. She believes he sees her as a dissident who is instilling rebellious ideas in the head of his only remaining daughter.

Despite the gloom that encompasses me at the moment, I laugh heartily when she says this. Little does my father know what ideas are in my head and how angry he will be when he finds out. But my rebelliousness has not come from Hild. I have arrived at my vow all on my own during my private discussions with God.

Hild tells me she emboldened herself and made a final plea to my father to allow me to accompany her to the north and enter her monastery. His answer had been short and firm. Her dismay is evident, but there is nothing more she can do.

Then, one day in the second week of May, a ship's man on a palfrey clatters up to the massive wooden doors of the great hall pulling a small cart behind him. While he is given refreshment in the kitchens, Hild and Gerda pack their meager belongings in their leather sacks and take them to the cart. I have been weeping in my chamber since the escort's arrival, but I know I must dry my eyes and say my farewells like the king's daughter that I am. I move toward the door just as father comes from his chamber followed, as ever, by Iurminus. King Cenwalh follows Iurminus. We all go out to the courtyard together, none saying a word.

The escort saunters out from behind the hall but steps smartly when he sees the women standing by the cart. Two of father's men, armoured atop their war horses, trot behind him. They come to a stop on either side of the cart. Father approaches Hild. She bows her head, and Gerda goes down to her knees.

"Thank you, Lord King Anna," says Hild, "for all your generosities these many months toward me and my companion. God bless you and all within your kingdom and grant you peace and prosperity."

"You are most welcome, Lady Hild," father replies courteously. "And thank you for your blessing."

Hild turns to Cenwalh. "I hope that you will soon be restored to your kingship in Wessex and that you will have a long and prosperous rule."

Cenwalh nods and replies, "Thank you, Lady Hild. I wish your new life to bring you joy and fulfillment."

Father points to his guards and says, "These two men will accompany you to the ship and bring me word that you are safely on board." He hands her a small package. "Here is a writ under my seal for your travels. I hope it will ensure your safe arrival in your homeland."

He hands her the writ wrapped in oiled cloth to avoid water damage as they traverse the marshes and fens between Rendlesham and the sea. Father steps back and Hild motions for me to come over. She wraps me in the folds of her cloak and whispers in my ear.

"Have courage, my child, and keep the faith. God will provide for you just as he has for me. Of this I am sure. Write to me whenever you are able, and I will do the same."

I nod and notice through my tear-filled eyes that Freyda has followed me out to the yard and is embracing Gerda, both sobbing a tearful farewell. Absorbed as I have been in my own misery, I have not thought to realize that Freyda is also losing a friend.

"How will I know where to send a letter?" I sniff, trying to hold back the flood of tears that threatens to burst free.

"I will send a missive to you when I am settled. It may be some time before you receive something but do not think I have forgotten. For the remainder of our lives on earth, you will never be far from my heart."

The women step up into the small cart and settle themselves on the narrow boards. It will be a painful, jostling journey to the coast. Perhaps Gerda will welcome the gentle rolling of the sea by the time they arrive at the ship. The escort mounts his horse and urges the animal forward with a boot heel to the ribs. He is dwarfed by the men on war horses on either side of the cart. I feel a sudden rush of affection for my father for sparing these men to assure the women's safe arrival at the ship.

Father, Iurminus, Cenwalh, Freyda and I stand there on the cobbles until the little party has disappeared from sight.

As we turn our backs and reenter the hall, I ignore the restraints of class and put my arm around Freyda's trembling shoulders to comfort her and resolve in my mind to be more thoughtful in the future of the people who share my life.

THE MIDDLE YEARS

Being comprised of letters between Hild and Etheldreda

During the years of our Lord 651 and 664

Letter One

October, in the year of our Lord 651
To my dear child and beloved friend,
Etheldreda, Princess of East Anglia
From Hild, Abbess of Hartlepool, Northumbria

I write to you, my dear Dreda, in the hope that you are healthy in body and, if not happy, at least content in spirit. At this moment, my spirit is a complexity of unmitigated joy and profound sorrow. As you read in my greeting, I am now the abbess of the monastery at Hartlepool, which situation has rewarded me with joy unbounded. But, to my sorrow, my beloved mentor, Aidan, Bishop of Lindisfarne, has left this earthly realm and ascended to the company of saints who live with God in highest heaven. I am, of course, overjoyed that he has received his heavenly reward for his good works and saintly life while on earth. However, I shall sorely miss his guidance and his deep understanding of the wisdom and meaning of the scriptures. He was a man of great compassion and humility who lived only to help people accept the mysteries of the faith. He owned nothing and what was given to him, he quickly gave away to others in need.

His last days were not happy ones, I am sorry to say. My homeland has been torn asunder with hostility between King Oswiu of Bernicia and King Oswine of Deira. The lesser nobles are rebelling and the Mercian demon, Penda, has resumed scourging the countryside. Life in the north is perilous and often short and miserable. In August of this year, Oswiu ordered the execution of his rival, Oswine.[44] *I tell you all of this because Bishop Aidan, although very close to Oswiu, also treasured his warm relationship with Oswine and I believe his heart was broken over the betrayal and murder of one dear friend by another. The proof of this is that Aidan passed to God only twelve short days after Oswine. He was staying at Bamburgh on an estate of Oswiu at the time of his passing and was buried in the graveyard at Lindisfarne.*[45]

When first I arrived in my homeland, Bishop Aidan gave to me a small plot of land on the River Wear where I lived with a few close companions for some months. Then the bishop called me to be the abbess here at Hartlepool. The need for a new abbess arose when the former, Heiu, left the monastery and went to live in another place. She was the first in Northumbria to be consecrated by the bishop to become a nun.[46] *Since coming here, I have been solely occupied with bringing a regular monastic system to our lives.*[47] *I have been helped in this by Bishop Aidan and other religious men who visit here. This is a double house of the kind that we talked about. Both men and women live in the monastery in strictly separate quarters after the custom in the monasteries of Francia.*

I am very anxious for news of you and hope with a full heart that this missive will find you. I am entrusting it to some pilgrims who will stop in Rendlesham. If you are no longer there, I hope your father will see that you receive it. Surely he has forgiven my former impertinence by now. I will wait patiently for a reply in your hand, which I know may be some months in coming. Perhaps God will provide a conduit for your letter before too long.

God bless you and keep you, my dear child.

Your loving friend, Hild

Letter Two

Spring, in the year of our Lord 653
To Mother Hild, Abbess of Hartlepool in Northumbria
From Etheldreda, Princess of the Island of Ely and Lady of
the South Gyrwas

My beloved Hild,

At last, your letter has found me. I am overjoyed to hear news of you and to know that your decision to return to Northumbria has rewarded you with the contentment of the monastic life that has, thus far, been denied to me. But do not fret for, at the moment, I am happy in my life.

After you left Rendlesham, father began to treat me more as an adult, allowing me to read to him and to discuss matters of religion. He in turn spoke to me of his fears for our kingdom, which had once again attracted the evil gaze of Penda. King Cenwalh of Wessex, who you will remember was in exile with us at Rendlesham, left us shortly after your departure and regained the kingship of Wessex. Eventually, I think it was two years ago, our family went back to Exning where I grew up and where father had been the general in charge of defending the dykes in the time of

King Sigeberht and King Ecgric. Messengers had warned him of the impending threat from Penda, and he wished to make sure the dykes were strong and war-worthy. I became reacquainted with your nephew, Ealdwulf, there. It will warm you to know that he is a very fine young man and a trusted warrior.

In the meantime, father was constantly occupied with finding a husband for me whose alliance with our family would be a help in the present threat and in the future. Eventually, he settled into negotiations with a Christian Ealdorman of the South Gyrwas,[48] Tondberht, by name. He is much older than I and when I was assured that he would be content solely with my companionship, I readily agreed to the union. He has kept his word and is gentle and considerate toward me. His morning gift to me was the island of Eels, and I am henceforth to be known as Princess of the island of Ely.[49]

My husband's worth to my father is not so much that he commands a great army, but the Gyrwas are sworn allies of the Wuffingas. Their lands, some 1200 hides,[50] are situated such as they may issue early warnings of impending raids by hostile Mercians.

My life in Tondberht's home is agreeable and, indeed, even pleasant. I have some duties as the Lady of the Gyrwas but am otherwise free to pursue my studies and delve more deeply into the scriptures. It is not unlike my life at Rendlesham as I seem to have traded one benevolent father for another. As well as my books and my two best gowns and cloaks, father allowed me to bring my mother's pendant and two other fine pieces that he had crafted for me in gratitude for my compliance regarding the marriage union. As

Tondberht's hall is more rustic than Rendlesham, and his guards even less civilized than my father's, I do not have much occasion to wear my jewellery. My chambers consist of two rooms, one for sleeping and the other for various activities. I confess I am given to wearing my jewellery in my chambers for no other reason than it pleases me to do so. I know this is vanity and I continually pray to our Saviour to take this sin away from me.

As I write, the messenger who will take this letter north is waiting to leave, so I must close now. May you continue to enjoy the felicity of God's work in your homeland and think of me from time to time as your devoted friend.

Etheldreda, Princess of the Island of Ely

Letter Three

December, in the year of our Lord 655
To Mother Hild, Abbess of Hartlepool
From Etheldreda, Princess of the Island of Ely

Oh, dear Mother,

I am distraught. There are no words dreadful enough to tell you of the sorrow that has gripped my soul. I long to have you here with me to help me through this heart-wrenching time.

Last year, my beloved father and brother were both butchered on the battlefield at Bulcamp near Blythburh by Penda, that dreadful scourge of this nation.[51] *Their heads were impaled on stakes at Rendlesham, and their bodies buried at Blythburgh. I cannot bear thinking of it. Poor Iurminus wanted so much to grow up to be a strong warrior and a good king like our father. When the news reached me here at Ely, I was struck down with grief and lay in my chamber for weeks, I know not how many, before I could summon the strength to be in the company of others. My mind tells me that I should be happy that my father and brother are free from all earthly cares and that they are enjoying their reward in the arms of our Saviour for their good lives on earth, but my sorrowing heart is broken, and it is too difficult to think in that way at the moment.*

My father's brother, Æthelhere, was made ruler of East Anglia under Penda's command. During those long dark nights in my chamber when my soul was bedevilled with all manner of horrific notions, it passed through my mind to wonder if my uncle had been involved in some treachery regarding my father. I do not know why I think this, and I have no knowledge of untoward actions by him, but he was always a man who was too much attracted to power. After the battle, he appeared to be on unseemly good terms with Penda, who had brought so much grief to my homeland and to yours.[52]

But you will know, as you read this, that our Blessed Saviour and our Lord has, at last, seen fit to rid this world of Penda and my uncle, his comrade in arms, and many Mercian warlords through the heroic actions of your king, Oswiu.[53] *Word of this great victory has reached us only recently so we have no details. We have prayed for the burden of this pagan scourge to be removed from us for so long that now that it has happened, we wonder how our little kingdom will go on. My beloved East Anglia will now be a vassal kingdom to Northumbria, and our king at the mercy of the whims of King Oswiu. We are fortunate that he is a Christian man. I know, dear Hild, that I should not have prayed for the death of another human being, but Penda was like a rabid beast all his life and, therefore, was less than human in my mind. I think God will forgive me.*

But now I come to the most recent misery to be inflicted on my fragile heart and soul. My dear husband, Tondberht, who has always been so kind and gracious to me, passed into the heavenly kingdom only a few days ago.[54] *I am left in my new land with no father, no brother, and no husband to protect me. I want nothing more dearly now than to enter your house and take my vows but, I fear as before that I will not be allowed to do that. The new King of East Anglia will be looking to me for another alliance, one that may not be as acceptable as my first.*

The one true light in my life at this moment is my friend and steward, Ovin, a man of mature years who was trusted in all things by my husband and who has been much help to me. I am very grateful that God has given him to me to lean on in my times of need and to trust with the affairs of my properties and duties to the people of the Gyrwas.

Please pray for me and for my sorrowing heart that I might let loose my burden and find a way to serve God and his Kingdom here on earth.

Etheldreda, Princess of the Island of Ely

Letter Four

November, in the year of our Lord 657
To Etheldreda, Princess of the Island of Ely
From Hild, Abbess of Whitby

My Dear Dreda,
You will be surprised to read that I am now the abbess of a monastery at Whitby, which is happily situated on an outcropping of land close to the sea where the air is fresh and our kitchen gardens flourish. But more of that another time.
First, I wish to attend to the monstrous and tragic events of the last few years. Mine, too, was a sorrowful heart when I learned of the death of your father and brother. Although we had our differences of thought, I always knew him to be a good Christian man and a strong and beloved leader. The people of East Anglia have lost a great soul. For all his Christian ways and beliefs, he was a man of his time and you might take some comfort in God's allowing him and Iurminus glorious and honourable deaths on the field of battle. It was what your father would have wanted for himself although, I suspect he would have preferred to be the warrior who ridded this country of the devil-beast, Penda.

But we must give thanks to our Lord that Oswiu at last prevailed at the Winwæd, and Penda and his warlords stride no more upon this earth. November 15 in the year of our Lord 655 will be a date that will forever cause the angels to sing.[55] *And those of us on earth can contemplate the eternal suffering that Penda will endure in the hell of the damned as a reminder that we must ever be just and compassionate and do good works in our expectation of a heavenly reward.*[56]

King Oswiu offered tribute to Penda and many other inducements for peace, but the devil refused because he was determined to crush the Northumbrian people and so, in this manner, brought about his own fate. The Mercians were a superior force in numbers, but King Oswiu made a vow to God that if he and his army were to prevail against Penda, he would endow twelve more monasteries and place his infant daughter, Ælfflæd, in a convent as a virgin dedicated to God. He was true to his word, and he and his queen, Eanflæd, daughter of our sainted King Edwin of whom you have heard me often speak, came in person to Hartlepool with Ælfflæd, who was entrusted to me. The king requested a private time with me and told me of all that I have written here. The queen passed this time with her infant, and there were many tears upon their parting. When I became abbess of this new monastic community at Whitby, Ælfflæd came with me. She is a dear child and beloved by all the nuns here.[57]

I am saddened for you by the death of your most satisfactory husband so soon after your marriage. I understand that you feel quite alone without a father, brother, husband, or kin to protect you. I would praise God if you were allowed to come here to Whitby[58] to take your vows, but I believe you are right in thinking that God still has other plans for your life.

Try to be patient, my child, and trust in the Lord on high and your steward, Ovin, here on earth.

God, in his mercy, grant you comfort in this uncertain time.

Your devoted friend, Hild

Letter Five

Spring, in the year of our Lord 659
To Mother Hild, Abbess of Whitby
From Etheldreda, Princess of the Island of Ely

My Beloved Friend,

I have momentous news, which brings both joy and terror to my heart. Our new king, Æthelwald, another of my father's brothers, has arranged a marriage for me with King Oswiu's son, Ecgfrith, who has had only fifteen winters and I a woman of twenty-nine. Once again, I am to be given like a chattel by one man to another. My royal birth ill protects me from the intrigues and schemes of the men who have power over me. Æthelwald insists it is my duty to my kingdom to help bind the alliance between King Oswiu and East Anglia, which has become, sadly, little more than a vassal state to Northumbria. But, now that my people are the Gyrwas and my home is here in Ely, I do not feel such a sense of duty. Besides, I know he is using me to strengthen his own power. At first, I refused outright because my sorrowing heart was repulsed by the idea. I want only to be left alone to my devotions and prayers. Ovin sees to my duties and affairs as princess of the Gyrwas, and I have trust in him. But your King Oswiu has made my marriage to his son a condition of peace and so, I am to be sacrificed yet again.

My beloved sister, Seaxburga, came to visit me a few weeks ago. She had travelled to Mercia with her daughter, Ermenilda, whose marriage to King Wulfhere,[59] younger son of Penda, had been arranged. She was able to satisfy herself that Wulfhere is a strong king and a good man of the faith, nothing like his father, and that her daughter will be well treated as queen of Mercia.

While she was here, my sister and I talked one night long after the tallows had guttered and the moon was our only light about my marriage to Oswiu's son.[60] She knows my heart and that I am inconsolable in this matter. Nevertheless, she tried to help me find some good in it. The chief good and only joy that I can find is the possibility of seeing you again if I am to make my home in the north. I am to leave for Bamburgh in a few weeks. I know not whether we travel by land or by sea, but if I am allowed any power over the decision, I will say by sea for I am told that we would pass close by Whitby on that route. I continue with my studies but your wisdom and guidance are sorely needed. Until now I had little hope of our meeting again but here, in his infinite love, God has instilled a hope in my heart that it will happen. If I am to pass my life in the north, perhaps there will be many opportunities to study and learn and talk with you.

I persist in this hope and in the faith that God will reward his humble and penitent servant.

Etheldreda, Princess of the Island of Ely

Letter Six

December, in the year of our Lord 660
To Abbess Hild of Whitby
From Etheldreda, Princess of Northumbria

My dear mother Abbess,

My wedding has come and gone and still I have not been allowed to see you. There was no ship to bring me close to Whitby on our journey. King Oswiu sent royal guards to escort us by a combination of cart paths and the old north-south Roman road. You know from your own experience how perilous that can be. My personal retinue consisted of my steward, Ovin, my loyal servant, Freyda, and two other women companions, all of the same hearts, as Christian as my own, and devoted to a life of contemplation and spiritual understanding.

I had little to bring with me because after Tondberht's death, I sold all my fine clothes and jewellery, except my mother's pendant, and gave what I received to the poor of Cratendune.[61] *My personal fortune now consists of the pendant and ten new gold coins, which I keep secreted among my meager belongings against the day I might have need of them. My arrival at King Oswiu's hall in my rough woollen robe drew astonished gasps from Queen Eanflæd and her ladies.*

At the beginning, I was overwhelmed in the presence of King Oswiu, who is given to much love of himself. His nature is large and dominating but, fortunately, he is not very interested in me except as a bride for his son. He is well aware of my vow of chastity and dedication of myself to God but seems convinced I will discard all that once I am married to Ecgfrith. And I am well aware that I find myself in this position merely because I am the only suitable princess from the south with whom to make an alliance. There is little doubt that the proud Oswiu would have preferred a match between Ecgfrith and my niece, Ermenilda of Kent, but his now sworn enemy, Wulfhere, King of Mercia, spoke first. And so, he had to make do with me, a woman who has vowed to remain chaste and, therefore, barren and unwilling to give his son children. It must gall him, but I believe he means to change my mind by whatever methods suit him.

Thus far, I have been well treated in your king's household though I find my new boy-husband's character to be somewhat strange. I blame his unusual behaviour on his boyhood circumstances. Do you know of this? When Oswiu became King of Northumbria, Penda was still his overlord by right of conquest and he would only allow Oswiu to assume the throne if he would give over his son as hostage to live at the Mercian court at Tamworth indefinitely. Ecgfrith was only a babe when he was taken away, so although he had two living parents, he was raised as an orphan in a land where the ruler was a pagan devil. I think he might have begun to hear of the true religion while in exile because, although Penda was a pagan, he did not banish Christianity from his kingdom. Indeed, as you probably know, his son, Peada, was baptized and converted when he married Oswiu's daughter, Alchflaed, an unfortunate choice for Peada, as it turned out.

Our marriage took place at York because it was thought the guests would be more impressed by the old Roman city than by the wooden castle at Bamburgh.[62] *We were married by Bishop Finan of Lindisfarne. I have agreed to keep up the pretense so as not to humiliate this child I find myself married to. Therefore, though the marriage is not consummated, I have accepted his morning gift of some land around the town of Hexham. Once again, I am in the position of defending my vow of chastity to God. I fear this husband may not be as agreeable as the last.*

I hope you will pray for me to find a way never to consummate this marriage.

Your loving daughter in spirit,
Etheldreda, Princess of Northumbria

Letter Seven

March, in the year of our Lord 662
To Etheldreda, Princess of Northumbria
From Hild, Abbess of Whitby

My Dear Dreda,

I have written many petitions to King Oswiu asking that you be allowed to visit me here at Whitby, but all my entreaties have fallen on deaf ears. His reluctance to allow us to renew our bond of friendship in person is a mystery to me. I believe it is more out of disinterest than malice. Or perhaps he sees in my early teachings, during our time in East Anglia, the source of your steadfast commitment to our Lord and your unwillingness to consummate your marriage. We know that you have made your vow out of your deepest desire to live with our Lord in humility and chastity, teaching his love wherever you travel. But Oswiu may still harbour hope that you can be persuaded to abandon your vow and provide him with a grandson and heir. I will continue my petitions on your behalf. Perhaps he will tire of my nagging and grant you leave to visit Whitby.

Life here in my monastery continues apace. I have many students under my care who are learning the value of a life dedicated to justice, piety, chastity, peace, and charity.[63] *It is the dearest desire of my heart that I and the other nuns may so deeply instill these values into the minds and souls of these young ones that when it is time for them to leave here, these principles will continue to guide their own lives and those whose lives are under their care.*

I hope that you are well in body and spirit, my dear young friend, and that you are content to believe that you are living the life that God has planned for you. I think of you with a loving heart and I pray for you.

Hild, Abbess of Whitby

Letter Eight

January, in the year of our Lord 664
To Hild, Abbess of Whitby
From Etheldreda, Princess of Northumbria

My dear mother, Hild,

What joyous news I have! Our loving God has seen fit to grant my heart's desire and prompted King Oswiu to include me in the royal party when we come to your monastery for the great meeting of churchmen.[64] I am as excited as were I the girl of seventeen years when we first met instead of the woman I am who has already achieved thirty-four winters.

I confess to you, in my darkest hours, I have committed the sin of abandoning hope that God would allow us to meet again but, in his great love, he has forgiven this poor sinner and bestowed this wonderful gift upon us.

I shall tell you how it came to be.

King Oswiu summoned Alchfrith[65] to come north from his court in Deira to Bamburgh. The king has been in an evil temper of late because Alchfrith, though born of an Irish mother,[66] has fallen in with Wilfrid and the Roman Christians and supports Queen Eanflaed in that cause.[67]

He has been ousting Irish churchmen in Deira who were given their positions by King Oswiu and installing Roman Christians such as Wilfrid in their place. This has caused much hard feeling between the church in Bernicia and that of Deira and between father and son.

I am aware, dear friend, that we stand on opposite sides in this controversy as well (solely because of the origin of our initiation into the faith), but I am determined not to be drawn into it. I can understand why there is such an uproar as it makes the royal family and also the Christian religion look foolish if the king, for instance, is celebrating Easter while the queen is celebrating Palm Sunday. This controversy has been festering for a long time but has attained a certain urgency as King Oswiu has been made aware that next year will bring the above circumstances into being once again. But you already know of this.

Ecgfrith has pronounced for his father and has been given permission to attend the conference. I will, of course, go as his wife. At last, some good will come of this miserable union for I will see you face to face once more. I hope we will have many hours to pass in conversation and study, but I fear that you will be much occupied with your abbatial duties during the royal family's time in your monastery.

Nonetheless, I anticipate with undiluted pleasure whatever time we will have together.

Your loving friend,
Etheldreda, Princess of Northumbria

THE GATHERING

Whitby Monastery, Northumbria, Britain

In the year of our Lord 664

Chapter Eight

I am engulfed once again in the great flowing robe of the abbess, Hild. I am a child again. Though she is shorter and a little rounder than I, she manages to gather all of me into herself just as she did when she left East Anglia those many years ago. My tears flow, and I taste their saltiness on her garment.

She rests her hands on my shoulders and holds me at arm's length, and I am able, at last, to look upon her face. Though she has advanced to the age of fifty years, the radiance of her skin and eyes has not diminished. Perhaps, it has even increased.

Queen Eanflæd is standing behind Hild and scowling at me. I realize suddenly that I leapt into Hild's welcoming embrace before giving her the opportunity to reverence me. I sometimes forget my royal status and think of myself only as a nun-in-waiting. I step back a pace or two, and Hild drops her head and bows slightly. I do not like her having to bow to me, but I accept it as I must many other unwanted aspects of my life.

I notice a young girl of about nine years shyly hanging back behind Hild, her eyes downcast.

"Ælfflæd?" I say tentatively, guessing that this is the infant that Oswiu and Eanflæd had left in Hild's care as a gift to God after Oswiu slew Penda in the momentous victory at the river Wineæd.

"Yes," she replies and bends her knee to me.

"Come, child, and greet your family." I encourage her in Eanflæd's direction.

She kneels to both parents and Eanflæd steps forward to pat her cheek.

"You have grown, child, since our last visit. Are you well and happy?"

"Yes, mother."

Hild steps forward and encircles Ælfflæd's shoulders with her arm.

"Your daughter thrives in our care, Highness, and is beloved by all of the sisters."

She turns and addresses our entourage.

"You are all most welcome here for this significant time of discussion. I am sure your long journey from north of the wall[68] has tired you."

"It was damnably long and gruelling," Oswiu mutters irritably.

"The bishops have all arrived," Hild says quickly, "and are resting in the cells provided for them in the men's dormitory. Sire, I have arranged lodging for you and your family in the hall of Lord Edgar less than half a league from here. You will be made most comfortable there. His man is waiting in the stable yard to show you the way. But I would beg a boon of you."

"Yes, what is it?" Oswiu asks, with the impatient air of a man whose only interest at that moment is to get to a place where his servant can tug off his riding boots and bring him a warm glass of good ale.

"I wish Princess Etheldreda to stay here with me. We are old and dear friends who have not seen each other in many years."

"What say you, Ecgfrith?" the king says to his son. "Can you manage three nights without your wife?"

"You know perfectly well, father, that I manage every night without my wife. Why should it be different here?" Ecgfrith replies indifferently. Then he adds ungallantly, "Besides, there is likely to be some tasty flesh among Lord Edgar's slaves."

Oswiu chooses to ignore his son's churlishness and turns to Hild. "You say all the churchmen from both sides are here so we might as well begin on the morrow. What hour?"

"I thought perhaps after Terce,[69] sire," replies Hild. "Will you break fast with us in the morning?"

Oswiu nods, turns on his heel and says, "Come, family. We will ferret out our guide in the stable."

They all troop obediently after the king. Ælfflæd has melted away somewhere. Suddenly, Hild and I are alone in the hall. Tears rush from my eyes again, and soon I am sobbing uncontrollably.

"Come, girl," Hild says, smiling kindly, "if you are going to sob during your entire time here, we will not have much of a visit."

"I'm sorry," I sniff. "I have been miserable for so long that this unexpected joy has overtaken my senses."

She takes me by the hand as though I were a child, which is how I feel, and says, "Come with me to the chapel. It is time to say None,[70] and afterward, we will go to your chamber, which is next to mine. You can rest while I prepare for the morrow."

Chapter Nine

Daylight is creeping away, and I am perched on the thin straw mattress covering the cot in my tiny cell. Freyda and Gerda have been reunited and are off somewhere together. Allowing both joy and sorrow to wash over me, I think on how fine it was at None to hear the nuns of Whitby singing, reading the psalms, and praying to our Lord. I know in my soul that this is the life I was born for but which, sadly, I cannot seem to accomplish for myself.

During the quiet prayers in the chapel, I begged God to tell me why this is so. Is all in our lives just an accident of birth? Being a woman, even a royal woman, seems to offer no more choices in life than being a slave, except the food is more nourishing and plentiful and the garments less rough. And yet Hild is of royal blood, and she has managed to make the life she desires.

I am on the brink of descending into another torrent of tears and self-pity when I hear a light tap at the door to my cell. The door creaks open. Hild slides quietly into the room.

"How fare you now, child?" she inquires carefully. "Has the flood subsided and are we on dry ground?"

"Just barely," I answer. "Oh, Hild, I am so happy to be with you here in your monastery. I cannot even think of leaving."

"Well, there is some time before you have to think of that," she says briskly, probably fearing I would start sobbing again. "Tell me about your life in Oswiu's court. Are you well treated?"

I nod without much conviction. "Mostly I am ignored. The queen is angry that I refuse to lie with her son and give her grandchildren. I fear every day that the king will force my husband upon me so there will be heirs. Ecgfrith, as you witnessed earlier, is often a childish brute given to tormenting small animals and women and any being weaker than himself, habits he no doubt learned while hostage in Penda's court.[71] But most of that is posturing and saving face. In spite of his behaviour, my heart is not hard toward Ecgfrith. If anything, I feel pity for him. How awful it must have been for him, a prince of the blood, to be reared in a pagan court far from his home. And then to return home to be forced into a marriage that was as unwelcome to him as it was to me.[72] We even seem to have forged a peculiar kind of friendship. Betimes, he comes to my chamber to sit and talk with me as one would to an older sister. It is during these times that my heart softens toward him, and I see him for the confused and unhappy man-boy that he is. Yet he is resolute that I shall not leave court and retire to religious life."

"I am sorrier than I can express that this life has been forced upon you. I have no words of consolation except to counsel you to remain steadfast in your faith and trust that for some reason unknown to us this is what God wants of you."

"Sometimes, I think I do not understand this God at all. Why would he want this life for me when I would be such a constant and willing worker for his kingdom on earth?"

"Again I can only say to you, child, that the ways of God are not always ours to understand. I believe all will be revealed in the end times but, until then, our faith must sustain and comfort us."

"I feel in danger daily of having my vow to God broken for me by the strength of people more powerful than I. I pray that if God does not will me to have the life I desire at this moment that he will at least give me the strength to hold firm to my vow of chastity."

"Does Ecgfrith threaten you in this regard?"

"He taunts me sometimes, but mostly he is too busy lying with slaves and his mistress, Eormenburga, who is one of the higher born ladies of the court.[73] I have begged him many times to release me to a monastery, but he stubbornly refuses. I know not why as I am of no use to him as a wife."

"I have no doubt it is because you are his father's hostage to keep your uncle in East Anglia in line. Perhaps when power shifts again, as it must, you will not be as useful, and you will be allowed the freedom of a monastery."

"That hope sustains me in my worst hours."

"Are you confirming that you have never once felt a small stirring of desire for your husband?"

I feel blood rushing to my face. "No, Mother, I have not. I have told you he is like a younger brother to me, like Iurminus when he lived."

"Is there a reason then why your face has reddened, and you do not lift your eyes to me?"

I shake my head and turn away.

She takes my hand and turns me back toward her. "Dreda, you must always tell me the truth. Have we not sworn this to each other?"

"Yes, Mother."

"Then tell me now what it is that you are ashamed to speak of."

"I am not ashamed," I protest. "But it is hard to tell you."

"Tell me what?"

"I had a dream one night just before our journey here. It was a most marvellous dream." My voice falters as the memory of the dream swallows me again.

"Go on, child," Hild urges me.

"I dreamed that our Saviour came to me," I blurt out, "and lay with me in the way a man lies with a woman."

Hild's face betrays her shock. I think this is not what she expected to hear. After a moment, she gathers herself and asks, "Are you saying that Jesus came to you in a dream and that he had carnal knowledge of you?"

"Yes."

She shakes her head. "I know not what to say."

"Nor I, Mother."

"Will you tell me about it?" she asks.

"I will try but I may not have the words to tell it properly." I pause for a moment and then begin as best I can to make her know what I felt. "In my dream, I am lying in my bed waiting for sleep. I feel some small movement in the air around me like a light summer wind except that I am inside my chamber so it cannot be the wind. I become aware of a man's unclothed body on the bed beside me. I know not how he came to be there, but I am not afraid. I look on his face, and I cannot see it clearly for the radiance. I know immediately it is Jesus."

"How did you know this?" Hild interrupts.

"I just did," I say and am surprised by the note of petulance in my voice. "After a few seconds of lying there, he shifted himself without effort and lay on top of me. There was no weight to his body and no substance. I could not touch him but I could feel him as he entered me. I was suddenly awash in a most wondrous feeling of pleasure and lightness. It was as though this whole horrible world had fallen into nothingness, and we two were all that remained."

I stop talking and we sit in silence for several minutes. I decide to wait until Hild speaks. Finally, she asks, "Did you waken while still dreaming?"

"I did. But the feeling persisted. It is with me still when I think about the dream."

"What did you do?"

"I tried to fall back into the dream, but I could not. Eventually I fell into a deep sleep and did not wake until dawn. When I rose from my bed, I noticed a stain on the bed linen. I became quite frightened because I did not want the bed servant to see the stain. After a bit, I fell on the idea of spilling some of the evening ale that still rested in my cup to cover up the stain."

"Was Freyda in your chamber during your dream?"

"She was but she sleeps like a dead horse. She heard nothing."

Hild shakes her head in wonder.

"We will speak of this again," she says, "but for now, I must think on this and we must pray on this dream in chapel. Now come child, it is time to share bread. For these few days, you may take part in our life here as though you were one of us."

Chapter Ten

The food board is made of three long, wide, rough-hewn boards from an oak tree, cradled at each end and in the middle by crossed stands. Sitting on the long benches amongst this community of women is a singular experience. I am determined to feel every precious moment of it. Two of the nuns appear with several bowls, which they lay down along the table. Some others bring in thick slabs of freshly baked bread. The aroma is enticing, and I wonder what it is, but we must wait until a psalm has been said and a hymn of thanks has been sung. The pure, sweet voices flow up to heaven as effortlessly here as they did in the chapel.

Hild signals the beginning of the meal by serving first me as their guest and then herself. The others serve themselves until everyone's bowl is filled. Unlike the boisterous table in Oswiu's hall, here no one speaks. For several minutes, the only sound is of wooden spoons knocking against wooden bowls. The pottage is a mixture of several vegetables probably uprooted from the kitchen garden this very morning. The cook must be a wizard with herbs because it is more delicious than any pottage I have tasted before, and I have had many opportunities upon which to base this observation.

I try to keep my eyes downcast as the nuns do, but it is an unfamiliar behaviour to me, and it becomes tiresome. It crosses my mind to wonder if any of them has lain with Jesus as I have. The meal is over quickly. We all exit in an orderly file to the chapel for Vespers,[74] leaving the cook and her helpers to gather up the bowls and the leftover bread and pottage. It occurs to me to hope that Freyda is being fed somewhere.

I am overcome once again by the holy air of the chapel. It seems to me as though God himself is standing in a corner watching the offices being read and sung. I want to find him and demand to know which of my former behaviours has sentenced me to the secular life, when all I have ever desired is the religious life. I cannot actually see him but I can feel his presence in this sacred space. I feel closer to him than I have ever felt. As I have been directed by Mother Hild, I pray for guidance and for a deeper understanding of my dream. I also pray that the memory of the dream and the feeling it arouses will be with me always.

After evensong is over, I wander down the corridor towards my cell, feeling as though a great gift has been bestowed upon me. I am calm and steadfast and no longer feel the floodgates threatening.

I hear footsteps behind me and turn to find Hild hurrying to catch up with me. She takes my arm and says, "Come with me, Dreda. I have something to show you."

As we walk along toward the hall, she remarks, "We have been so intent on the blessing of our reunion that we have not even discussed the gathering of the bishops."

"I don't suppose we will be asked to contribute to the deliberations," I say.

Hild laughs. "Unlikely," she agrees, "but the outcome is crucial to the church and I intend to listen to every word." She stops and pulls back a heavy drape to reveal a tiny closet surrounded by the same drapery. A small stool is the only furnishing.

"The hall where the churchmen will meet and deliberate is on the other side of this curtain. You may sit here and listen to the debate, but you must not make a sound. Can you do that?"

"I shall try. It will probably be so pompous and boring that I will go to sleep and fall off the stool."

"My dear," Hild trots out her scolding tone that I well remember from our days in my father's hall, "history will be made here tomorrow or the next day that will affect the church in Britain for all time to come. You'd best take it seriously."

"Yes, Mother," I say contritely. "May I ask on which side of the discussion you stand now though I believe I already know?"

"Of course. Though I was baptized by Paulinus in the Roman manner when I was a child, I have since, as you know, been a disciple of Aidan who followed the Irish traditions, and so I will support the Celtic argument."

"The same side as the king."

"As it happens but not for that reason. Come, Dreda, it is time for rest. I will see you at Vigils, Lauds, and Prime.[75]

After Prime, we must prepare the table and the kitchen for the bishops and the royal party, as they will break their fast here before Terce. The meeting will begin after the Offices of Terce.

Sleep eludes me. Freyda is snoring gently on her little pallet. It always astounds me how that girl can sleep anywhere. I do not want to miss anything, and I fear that I will sleep through Vigils if I allow myself to drift off. Surely, I tell myself, a little bell is rung throughout the convent. I wonder whose responsibility that is. Whoever it is must have to stay awake in order to wake the others on time. I decide that they probably take turns. That is my last thought until a bell is rung outside my cell door. Freyda does not stir, but I leap off my cot and pull on my cloak myself and pad along the cold stone floor of the corridor to the chapel.

Chapter Eleven

Breakfast is the same gloomy affair as supper had been the night before except for being much more colourful as the principals in the day's business have turned out in their richest vestments and regalia as befitting the importance of the occasion. If it is a contest among the bishops, the Romans win handily as their finery far surpasses the garments of the Irish bishops in regard to richness of material, colourful dyes, and bejewelled pins and belts. The representatives of the two traditions are also easy to discern by their tonsures.[76]

The royal party in turn surpasses all the bishops garbed as they are in deep burgundy ceremonial cloaks lined with fur of the wolf. Upon their heads sit golden crowns also transported from Bamburgh. This is in stark contrast to the plain brown wool robe that Ælfflæd is wearing. She has been given the privilege of sitting between her parents. She ignores her brothers whom she does not know and appears uncomfortable and self-conscious. I wonder what is in her mind as she sits between the two people who brought her into this world and then gave her away as though she were a trinket. Of course, I think she is the fortunate one. As an infant, she achieved without any effort the life that I have so desperately wanted since I was seventeen years of age.

Oswiu seems to have decided that all would honour the customs of the monastery and the bishops. Everyone consumes their ale and hard bread and cheese with no speech and eyes downcast, though I manage to spot a few glances between the bishops, and I notice Ecgfrith scowling at me from time to time.

When it is over, everyone repairs en masse to the chapel for Terce. King Oswiu is given the honour of reading the psalm, the nuns sing, and one of the bishops, whose name I do not know, recites the common prayers with a special prayer that the events of the day will be guided by the light of the all-knowing and all-loving God. Then the royal party and the bishops arise as one. Led by Hild, they parade down the corridor to the hall where the proceedings are to take place. I lag behind with the nuns, who are not allowed to attend, and then surreptitiously take my place in my little closet. I part the curtain just slightly because I want to be able to see as well as hear.

The debaters each are allotted a chair at the large round table in the centre of the hall. The bishops' entourages and other minor churchmen are seated on benches along the perimeter of the room. King Oswiu and Queen Eanflæd each sit in majesty at the head of the hall on large throne chairs that have been hauled by horse cart from Bamburgh. Ecgfrith sits on a smaller chair to the right of his father, and Alchfrith, the king's other son by his former wife and a Roman supporter, does the same to the left of the queen. The lines are drawn.

Chapter Twelve

Freyda is nowhere to be seen when I return to our tiny cell next to Hild's. I reckon she has been called to the kitchen with Gerda to help the nuns with the extra food preparation for the bishops and their companions.

I am lying on the thin straw pallet of my cot, failing miserably in coaxing some comfort for my sore bones. Hunching on the hard wooden stool in the little closet off the great hall for more than six hours has done my aching body no favour. To take my mind away from the pain, I am recalling the details of the debate and attempting to discern for myself which arguments were wheat and which were chaff.

When each person was settled into his allotted place, King Oswiu rose from his great throne chair. In his deep rumbling voice, he welcomed all in attendance to this solemn and sacred debate. He announced that God was displeased that Christians in Britain did not worship as one and had sent a sign by darkening the sun.[77] He explained the business of the day by saying that since we all worship the one true God and we all hope for the same kingdom of heaven, it is only right that we all celebrate the divine mysteries in the same fashion.

I thought at that moment that this was mighty holy talk from a man who out of the base desires of power and greed had cold-bloodedly ordered the murder of his cousin, Oswine, ruler of Deira, because he did not want to share the kingdom of Northumbria. Clearly his Christian principles did not govern all aspects of his life. Oswiu then retold the well-known story that, due to the differences between the Irish and Roman traditions, he and his queen, Eanflæd, were often forced to celebrate Easter, the most holy of all the rites, at different times. He then promised a just verdict at the close of the deliberations.

Bishop Colman of the Irish tradition was called to speak first. I remember wondering who decided who would speak first. Would it be an advantage given to the king's preference or would it even matter? After all, I had to believe that the true way would triumph because that would be the will of God. But I know from experience that, try as we might, true believers are not always able to discern the true will of God. Having offered up countless pleas and prayers to God regarding my own most earnest desire to become a bride of Christ, I still find myself burdened with earthly husbands. The will of God for my life remains shrouded in mystery.

When Bishop Colman lumbered to his feet, I was struck again by his humble appearance. His robe was brown sacking tied around the waist with rope from which hung an intricately carved wooden cross. I wondered vaguely if he himself were the carver. His demeanour suggested that he understood the depth of the responsibility that had been placed in his care. He was defending all that he and his fellow Irish Christians held sacred in this world.

The basis of his argument was fairly simple. He said that Irish tradition originated with his forefathers, Columba of Iona and Aidan of Lindisfarne, men who were beloved by God. He argued that the Irish way should not be rejected or considered contemptible because it is the same tradition followed by St. John the Evangelist, who was the disciple beloved of Jesus. He concluded with the rather circular argument that his tradition is the correct one in the eyes of God because it is the one observed in all the churches over which he, Colman, presides.

Although Colman exhibited a steely strength of belief in his tradition, I thought at the time that his argument was too weak and specious to prevail.

The pains in my body have eased somewhat and I feel I might drift into sleep, but I am forcing myself to remember the arguments for the Roman side before they become clouded in memory.

It seemed odd to me that Wilfrid, a mere priest, should speak for the Romans. But Agilberht, the bishop of the West Saxons, rose to explain that Wilfrid was chosen because he could better express himself in the English language. I noticed when he stood to speak that Wilfrid, the priest, wore a more costly and ostentatious garment than did Colman, the bishop.

Wilfrid's argument relied heavily on the idea that most everyone in the Christian world beyond our shores observes the Roman practice because it was the tradition of the blessed apostles, Peter and Paul. There was a ripple of bristling among the Irish contingent when Wilfrid accused the Picts and the Britons of obstinancy when, from their remote islands, they insisted on opposing the traditions of the whole rest of the Christian civilized world.

Colman sprang to his feet and asserted in barely measured tones that it was strange that Wilfrid would cast aspersions on the tradition of so worthy an apostle as was allowed to lay his head on the breast of Jesus.[78]

Wilfrid countered this idea with the argument that Colman and his people were not actually following the practices of St. John the Evangelist and that they were ignorant of the law and of the workings of the science of computus and, therefore, ignorant of the most sacred teachings of Holy Writ.

At these insults, Colman's humble demeanour slipped away and his face was contorted with anger, but each time he tried to speak, Wilfrid put forward another compelling argument to refute Colman and the Irish. He accused the Irish of reading apocryphal texts[79] that the Romans tried to supress and of being too attached to the old ways, allowing Irish Christians to honour the old gods.[80]

When Wilfrid dared to suggest that Colman and his fellow Irish bishops were in a state of sin if they continued to ignore the decrees of the Apostolic See and of the universal Roman church and the teachings of Holy Writ, I feared Colman was in danger of slipping into a fit and losing his senses.

At this point in the debate, I believe Wilfrid could smell victory and so imbued was he with the Holy Spirit and his own righteous argument that he pressed on heedless of the angry voices rising out of the Irish contingent.

At the height of his oratory, he asked Colman if Columba was to be considered more holy than Peter, the prince of the apostles? Then, without waiting for an answer, he began quoting the familiar words of our Lord in Holy Writ. "Thou art Peter, and upon this rock, I will build my church, and the gates of hell shall not prevail against it, and to thee I will give the keys of the kingdom of heaven."[81]

Colman sank to his chair, the full weight of imminent defeat pressing on his shoulders. At this point, King Oswiu interrupted Wilfrid's rhetoric and asked Colman if it were true that these words were spoken by our Lord to Peter.

Colman muttered, "It is true, sire."

"And was any such power given to Columba, the most holy of the Irish holy men," Oswiu inquired. "Or to John the Evangelist?"

Colman merely shook his head, unable to raise his eyes to the king.

Oswiu called for silence in the hall and then pondered for a few minutes. He rose to his feet to render his verdict. He said that he was saddened to learn that all his life he had not been practising the true way but would, henceforth, endeavour to follow the correct path in all things. His verdict was clear. He found for the Roman tradition on the grounds that if Peter were the doorkeeper of heaven, then he, Oswiu, would not contradict him and would in all things obey his decrees lest when he himself came to the gates of heaven, there would be none there to open them if he continued to be the adversary of him who held the keys.

All on the Roman side murmured their assent and resolved to conform to the more perfect tradition as decreed by their king.[82] The Irish contingent sat silent in defeat.

As I think on all of this, I am grateful that the king had the good sense to make a just and holy verdict. I decide to ignore the fact that his decision was almost wholly grounded in self-interest and decide instead to offer up prayers of thanksgiving to God for instilling wisdom in our king when he needed it most.

At last, I drift off into a light sleep but am awakened by a knocking at the door of my cell.

Chapter Thirteen

"Enter," I say and Hild comes in, her face sagging with the grief of bitter disappointment. She pulls a small stool, the only other piece of furniture in the room, over to the bed and sinks down upon it.

She takes my hand and says sorrowfully, "Well, child, it seems that you were schooled rightly after all, and I have been in error and sin these many years."

I am driven to console her. "That cannot be so," I say, "for there is no other person I know upon this earth who walks more closely with our Father and his Son."

A weary sigh escapes her. "We cannot allow that the king is in error on this point, though I doubt he has given over much time to contemplate it. I admit to profound disappointment over his decision. As you know, I have always held that the Irish tradition more closely reflects that of our Lord's disciples and of our Lord Jesus himself who walked humbly among the people with few garments or other possessions, unlike those Roman posturers who support Wilfrid's claim."

"For myself," I say, "I think that the king is correct in supporting St. Peter's tradition, but I also believe that

Christ's way would be better served if all its adherents lived and served in the manner of the Irish priests and bishops."

"Well said, child," Hild agrees, "but now that the Roman faction has been granted absolute authority by the king, I believe the Roman bishops will only become more elaborate in their clothing and more pompous in their preaching. They will consider themselves the final authority in all matters religious. The way of humility and love for one's fellow creatures will disappear in the hierarchy and become the way of power and expediency. Already, Wilfrid struts about the hall in the manner of one who has won a great victory, as I suppose he has," she says sadly.

"And Bishop Colman and his companions have departed in anger. Who knows what will become of them? Admittedly, Wilfrid may have had the stronger argument, but he wilfully and needlessly crushed and humiliated Colman. If that is the Roman way, I believe this day will someday bring great grief upon the people of God."

"What will you do?" I ask.

"What I must," Hild answers, shaking her head. "Oswiu's authority is not to be questioned, and so I will honour his decision in the celebration of the sacraments and the liturgy, but I will continue to teach my pupils the Irish way of humility, charity, peace, justice, piety, and chastity."

"As usual, your wisdom will prevail," I reply, in genuine admiration for this woman whom we all call mother.

"That remains to be seen," she replies archly. "I fear this day that Wilfrid has made in me a great enemy. I shall have to pray diligently to find a way to remove the bad feeling for him from my heart. But there is now another issue to be dealt with."

"What is that?"

"The question of the monks' tonsure. There will be much bitter grumbling, I expect, when I and other abbesses of double houses based on the Irish tradition try to compel Roman tonsure on our monks."[83]

"Is there no choice in this?"

"No. You heard King Oswiu dictate that we will henceforth follow Roman tradition in all respects. This debate was not solely about the computing of the Easter date. It was really about establishing the domination of the Roman way. You know that it was Alchfrith, goaded by Wilfrid, who urged this meeting on his father."[84]

"How do you know this?" I ask, astonished.

"Would you think less of me if I admitted I listened in to a conversation between Alchfrith and Wilfrid?"

"Of course not." Then a thought occurs to me. "It will take some time to grow the hair needed to switch from the Irish to the Roman tonsure," I observe, returning to the issue at hand.

Demonstrating that some of her usual good nature is returning, Hild remarks, "It will also present a hardship for some of the older monks who are naturally bald and cannot grow hair on the forehead to complete the crown. I wonder what the rules say about this situation? The Irish tonsure is much easier in this regard as it follows the more natural balding pattern for men."

We both smile at this possible predicament and the mood lightens a little.

"Presumably, the Romans have established a rule for this issue as they have for all other aspects of Christian life," Hild remarks and then changes the subject. "Now, Dreda, we must speak further regarding your dream. I have been praying to our Lord for guidance, and I believe I have come to some understanding of it. Although your dream seemed to you to be of a carnal nature, I think, my dear child, that you have been the recipient of a miracle. I believe the Holy Spirit has come to you and invested you with its light."

"Do you believe then that I have not lain with Jesus?" I ask, my disappointment evident. "What about the stain on the bed linen?"

"I believe that in the dream it seemed to you that you were in intercourse with Jesus but, dreams are not to be taken literally no matter how much we may wish it. If that were so, it would mean in my mother's dream that she would give birth to an actual jewel rather than to me whom she considered a jewel. As for the stain, it may be explained that in your ecstasy your own body involuntarily released some of its sexual fluid."

I feel on the verge of tears again. I wanted desperately for it to really be Jesus coming to me, his humble servant.

"But do not look so downcast, child," Hild scolds. "It is no small thing to receive the miracle of the Holy Spirit. I believe it is a sign that God's plan for your religious life is soon to be made manifest and that great joy is ahead for you."

"Oh, Mother, do you really believe so?" I cry with sudden excitement.

"I do, with my whole heart," she replies. "But now, we must go to the food hall. The king and his companions are dining here tonight and attending Vespers thereafter, presumably to thank God for bestowing upon him the clarity of vision that resulted in his Roman choice," she adds wryly. "I must admit that all this hospitality is putting a strain on our already struggling coffers. This evening's meal will be far less elaborate than they will be expecting."

"Does the king not help in this regard?"

"Not thus far but perhaps he will leave something before he departs."

A heavy weight falls once more on my shoulders and in my heart.

"When do they leave?" I ask, attempting to suggest that the company might depart without me.

"They will hunt on the morrow. The next day, they will meet with some of the great lords hereabouts and then leave the morning after that. You will accompany them," she replies, laying a hand of comfort on my shoulder.

I know in my heart that this is the way it has to be but still I beg of Hild, "Can you not persuade the king and my wretched husband to allow me to stay with you?"

"I have tried, child. I accosted the king in the hall after the deliberations, hoping his mood would be generous, and asked if you might stay here with me if only for a few days longer, but he and Ecgfrith both refused to hear of it."

The tears that I had held back this whole day flood forth again, and I shake uncontrollably. Hild gathers me to her, uttering words of comfort that we both know are inadequate. After awhile, she starts praying for me and my desperate situation. She asks God to relieve me of this burden of marriage and the secular life. Her praying calms me enough to think about going to the evening meal. I wash my face hoping the basin's cold water will shrink the puffiness from my eyes.

Once again, I face the desolation of my life, but this time is different. I will leave with the hope that Hild has rightly interpreted my dream and that God is ready for me to devote my life and work to his kingdom on earth. And I still have two days here in the monastery to learn more of the life I am praying will soon be mine.

THE DESPERATE YEARS

Being comprised of letters between Hild and Etheldreda

During the years of our Lord 664 and 672

Letter Nine

Autumn in the year of our Lord 664
To Abbess Hild of Whitby
From Etheldreda, Princess of Northumbria

My Dear Mother Hild,

What a joy it was to see you earlier this year! Unfortunately that lightness of heart our visit instilled in me has been tempered by having to leave you and by sad news from Kent. King Eorconberht fell ill during the great pestilence[85] and died last 14 of July. You will remember he was the husband of my beloved sister, Seaxburgh. This will be a very hard blow for her since he was a loving husband and gave her a stable and secure life. The messenger reported also that their son, Ecgberht, is now king in Kent. Seaxburgh has retired to the convent at Minster-In-Sheppey, which she had previously founded. I know she will eventually find joy there.

Our visit to Whitby has altered nothing for me at court. Everyone ignores me, and I pass among them as though I were a shadow. I barely attract the notice of a single person.

But since my dream, I am a different person now. I wait in hope instead of falling into despair.

King Oswiu has decided on Wilfrid to be bishop of York, but he has gone to Francia to be consecrated and may be away for some time. Meanwhile Oswiu has chosen Chad to be bishop until Wilfrid's return.[86] *He is a good man, a pupil of Aidan, as you probably know. I believe Chad's appointment will be good news to you, if it is indeed news. Perhaps you already know of these events. My steward, Ovin, of whom you have heard me speak is much taken with Bishop Chad and would in his heart wish to be a disciple of his. I think his loyalty to me inhibits him. I would like to let him go but, in truth, I cannot as, except for the women who serve me, he is my sole support and only friend in this loveless place.*

Your loving daughter-in-Christ,
Dreda

Letter Ten

Spring in the year of our Lord 666
To Etheldreda, Princess of Northumbria
From Hild, Abbess of Whitby

My dear Dreda,

I am sorry I was unable to write to you these many months, but it was for a very good reason. The most holy of holy events has transpired in my monastery. We have had a genuine miracle! And as ever with public miracles, many religious personages must be consulted and much talk and dithering about must occur. At last, all has been settled and the miracle deemed true and rooted in a gift of the Heavenly Father. I shall tell you about it.

Among the folk who work in and around the monastery is a certain herdsman named Cædmon. He is a simple, unschooled man who has worked most of his years in the secular world and has now achieved a great age. This is his testament as told to me and many learned men who were summoned to hear his story.

One night, he had been carousing in a mead-hall with some of his fellows and, as often happens, they decided to entertain themselves by playing instruments and offering songs. Feeling humiliated about not knowing any songs, Cædmon left the hall and went to the stable where he was to care for the horses that night.

While in a deep sleep, a person appeared to him asking him to sing. He replied that he could not sing, but the person insisted he sing about the beginning of creation. Presently he began to sing verses that he had never heard before. When he awoke, he could remember all he had sung and went to tell the steward who then brought him to me.

I was astounded and brought to tears to hear these beautiful words spring from the mouth of so lowly a soul. Immediately, I brought Cædmon to the scriptorium to have his words written down. And then, I sent word to the priests and bishops to come, for I recognized that God was truly speaking through this man. They too were astonished and tested him by reading to him passages of Holy Writ and then sending him away to compose the same thing in verse. He returned each time with the most excellent verse and all agreed that this was truly a divine gift from God and a genuine miracle.

I have been able to convince Cædmon that he should leave his cow herding and join the brethren in my monastery. When he agreed, I ordered the brethren to teach him all that they were able of sacred history in order that we might have more verses from him. He is with the brethren now and composing many verses concerning the stories of the Old Testament.[87] *I will tell you now the words of his first miracle so that you may study them and your spirit may be raised up by them.*

Nu sculon herigean / heofonrices Weard
[Now must we praise / heaven-king-dom's Guardian,]

Meotodes meahte / and his modgeþanc
[the Measurer's might / and his mind-plans,]

weorc Wuldor-Fæder / swa he wundra gehwæs
[the work of the Glory-Father, / when he of wonders of every one,]

ece Drihten / or onstealde
[eternal Lord, / the beginning established.]

He ærest sceop / ielda bearnum
[He first created / for men's sons]

heofen to hrofe / halig Scyppend
[heaven as a roof, / holy Creator;]

ða middangeard / moncynnes Weard
[then middle-earth / mankind's Guardian,]

ece Drihten / æfter teode
[eternal Lord / afterwards made –]

firum foldan / Frea ælmihtig.
[for men earth, / Master almighty.][88]

I am humbled beyond measure that our Lord has seen fit to visit a miracle upon a person in my keeping. I hardly know what to do. Cædmon's renown is spreading throughout the north, and yet he continues to live simply, tending the animals and studying with the brothers of the monastery.

His gift came upon him so suddenly, he himself seems almost dumbstruck except when he is singing and composing.

Be well, my dear friend. In the unlikely event the news of Cædmon has not yet reached the court, you may be the first to relay it to the king.

Your loving mother in Christ,
Hild

Letter Eleven

Summer in the year of our Lord 670
To Hild, Abbess of Whitby
From Etheldreda, Queen of Northumbria

My dear mother Hild,

You will not be surprised to see written my most recent title, Queen of Northumbria, as you will no doubt know of the death of King Oswiu in February of this year. Ecgfrith has been crowned king at York and I his queen though, as you know, in name only.

When I learned that Oswiu's queen, Eanflæd, had decided to retire to your monastery to join her daughter, Ælfflæd, I took the opportunity to urge one of her servant girls to bring this missive to you. I have aided the girl and her family on occasion and so, I am being repaid with her gratitude.

Life at court has been strangely quiet since Oswiu's death. Except for public occasions when royal decorum dictates that I be at his side, Ecgfrith continues to flaunt his mistress and his other conquests in some sort of vain hope that I will relinquish my vow. As I have managed to pass my fortieth winter, I will hardly give it up now. But Ecgfrith is twenty-five and at the height of his powers. I do understand that I present him with a confounding problem that brings out the fury in him.

Of course, you know that he wants me to consummate our marriage merely to have a legitimate heir out of me. His nobles have been bringing more and more pressure to bear on him, making his moods more volatile than ever. They are saying that our situation disgraces him and weakens him in their eyes. This is terrible to hear because there is nothing Ecgfrith covets more than the regard of his nobles. His deepest aspiration is to emulate his father as a strong, respected, Christian king.

I hesitate to mention this because I know your strong dislike of Wilfrid has not lessened since the days of the great gathering, but he has become very powerful once again after enduring several years of disfavour, the ins and outs of which are too complicated for me to understand. It is sufficient for me that he is now Bishop of York and has been establishing monasteries all over Northumbria. I myself have promised him my dower lands at Hexham.[89] But I mention Wilfrid because he has become a great friend to me at court. I don't need to tell you that he is in the minority in this regard, especially as I have released my stalwart steward, Ovin, to go to Bishop Chad at Lastingham. Ovin has now followed the bishop to Lichfield.[90] In good conscience, I could no longer deny him the religious life he wanted so desperately even though our Lord sees fit to deny it to me. Wilfrid has the ear of the king and has agreed to try to convince Ecgfrith to allow me to retire from court and enter a monastery. I pray every waking moment that he will be successful and that I will be allowed to come to you at Whitby, even though I know that there I shall have to endure the scowls and bad temper of his mother.

Pray for me, dear mother,
Etheldreda

Letter Twelve

Autumn in the year of our Lord 671
To Etheldreda, Queen of Northumbria
From Hild, Abbess of Whitby

My dear Dreda,

Ever since Queen Eanflæd has taken up residence here in Whitby and has had the body of Oswiu and the bones of her father, King Edwin, interred here, life has become very busy.[91] *We are constantly visited by pilgrims and many royal and religious personages. Some of the latter have even consulted me on some thorny matters of state and difficult scriptural passages having received the notion that my wisdom might be superior to their own. Some have even asked me for my opinion on the great mortality of birds that our land is experiencing.*[92] *I have had to confess that this catastrophe is beyond my understanding.*

Apparently, much has been heard in the kingdom and beyond of the virtues of justice, piety, and charity that we observe here in strict obedience to the teaching of the Holy Scriptures and of our Lord. Indeed, five of our brethren have been consecrated bishops throughout the country. It has pleased God to bless us with these honours.[93] *The medical arts practised by my nuns and myself have also become well known. We are regularly visited by patients whose conditions are regarded as hopeless by other healers. Through the grace of God, we have ofttimes been able to secure a remedy or at least a remission for these unfortunates. Ælfflæd seems particularly gifted in this regard.*

It may gratify you to know that Queen Eanflæd, though still a powerful personality, has taken to our simple life here at Whitby and appears to be most joyful to be reunited with Ælfflæd. She has even confided to me that, though it does not please her, she understands your situation and hopes for some resolution if only for the sake of her son and the continuation of the Northumbrian royal house.

It saddens me to hear that your only ally is Wilfrid because I still believe that Wilfrid's own interests will always come above all others. However, it may be that your interests and Wilfrid's coincide, and you will be able, through him, to find a way to bring about your dearest wish.

I continue to pray for you at every moment.

Your loving mother in Christ,
Hild

Letter Thirteen

December in the year of our Lord 672
To Mother Hild, Abbess of Whitby
From Sister Etheldreda, nun of Coldingham

Dear Mother Hild,
I have no doubt you will be astonished by my new title. I sometimes cannot believe it myself. Our loving Father has, at last, taken pity on this poor servant and has granted the dearest wish of my heart.

As I told you in my last missive, Wilfrid has continued to press my cause upon the king. I know not why because from what I have learned, it has cost him dear. My spies at court tell me that Ecgfrith had promised Wilfrid a great many lands and large amounts of money if he could persuade me to give up my vow and consummate our marriage.[94] I have repeatedly told Wilfrid that God has lit a fire in my spirit that cannot be quenched. Perhaps his conscience as bishop has pricked him into standing by me and my vow of chastity,[95] and so he has continued to pressure Ecgfrith to release me from the marriage. Knowing Wilfrid, I am certain that there were other reasons that will be to his benefit, but I do not wish to be apprised of them. I wish only to revel in the joy I have found in my new life due to whatever manipulations he employed to achieve this precious situation.

When this moment at last arrived, my whole heart wished to come to you at Whitby, but here Ecgfrith drew the line. His permission to retire was contingent upon my coming to Coldingham where his aunt, Æbba, is the abbess.[96] I believe he thinks Whitby too far away and he fears your influence in the religious world. Although he has permitted my departure from court, I do not feel secure since Coldingham is only a fast ride of two days northward along the coast and Ecgfrith's men could easily retrieve me from here.

On this point, I console myself that surely Ecgfrith would not break the sanctuary of a nun who has received her veil and her clothing from the hands of Bishop Wilfrid himself.[97] However, I do believe that Ecgfrith was worn out by the continual petitions from Wilfrid on my behalf and the harassment and pressures from his nobles to do something about his situation. When he is in a stronger position, he could easily change his mind.

As soon as he gave in to Wilfrid, my ladies and I, including Freyda, left all our possessions in Bamburgh. I brought only my gold coins, my mother's pendant, my hoard of parchment and your beloved letters.[98] We made our way on a horse and donkeys along the coastal tracks to Coldingham. It was a brisk journey of two and a half days. The villagers along the way gave us food and shelter.[99] We have been warmly welcomed by Æbba and her community of both nuns and monks.

The monastery itself is nearly totally cut off from the outside world and the winds howl almost without remission. It is a perfect place for me to practise my devotions and daily prayers giving thanks to Almighty God for this bountiful blessing given to me in the forty-second year of my life. In gratitude for his unceasing efforts on my behalf, I have now legally granted my land at Hexham to Wilfrid for the purpose of building a church and a monastery there.

Your ecstatic daughter in Christ,
Etheldreda

FLIGHT FROM NORTHUMBRIA

Chapter Fourteen

Urgent rapping at my cell door startles me from my night prayers. Mother Æbba rushes in without waiting to be bidden, and I can tell from her high colour that something is amiss.

"What is it, mother?" I ask, alarmed by her behaviour.

"A pigeon has arrived. Someone in the court is a friend to you and has warned us that Ecgfrith and his nobles are coming for you. There is not a moment to lose. You must be ready to flee within the hour or sooner. I will find Freyda and your women and Ovin and tell them."

I stand riveted to the ground by shock and fear.

Æbba shakes my shoulders gently. "Come, daughter, there is no time for this. If you do not escape now, you will be taken to Bamburgh and Ecgfrith will make a proper wife of you, by force, if necessary."

"But why, mother? I am an avowed nun and a daughter of Christ. Why would he do this after releasing me?"

"Because he is a man and a king who is losing the respect of his nobles and because he can. He needs no other reason. Now come, child, gather your belongings and meet me in the stable yard. And dress warmly. There is a little nip in the air tonight."

Æbba hurries off.

I force myself into action. Tears trickle down my cheeks as I, once again, stuff my gold pieces, my mother's pendant, Hild's letters, and my dwindling stash of parchment into my oilskin bag. I put on my outside habit and cloak of heavy wool and pull on my leather boots. I secrete the bag and my book of scripture in the long inside fold of my cloak. I take a hasty look around my beloved tiny cell and close the door on it for what I suspect will be the last time.

As I hurry to the stables, it occurs to me to wonder why Æbba has ignored the laws of kinship and is helping me instead of her nephew. I do not know the answer, but I sense that I will always hold her in my prayers with my most profound gratitude.

When I reach the stable yard, Ovin, Freyda, and my two women, Sewara and Sewenna, who had come north with me from Cratendune,[100] are already there waiting for me. The stable boy has brought out the donkeys and the horse that we had consecrated to the monastery's use less than a year ago. Æbba and two other nuns are tying bundles to the donkey's backs with straps around their bellies.

"There is a little nourishment here for you," says Æbba, "but it will not last long. You will have to hope for kindness from strangers along the way. There are also some clothes that will disguise you if you need to put away your religious garments for a while. Do you have any idea of where you will go?"

"Yes, but perhaps it is better if you do not know, mother," I reply cautiously. "I fear Ecgfrith's wrath when he discovers what you have done."

"All will be well, daughter. We are each of us in the loving hands of our Father. Now, you must make haste. Ovin should mount the horse. I fear the little donkeys would sag under him."

"Mother, will you bless us on our journey?"

"Of course, child, come close." Æbba stands up on her toes to put her hand on my head. "Loving and all-powerful God, I earnestly ask that you and your beloved son will bless these faithful workers for your kingdom on their journey. If it be your will, keep them from harm and see them safely to their destination. Hear my prayer and have mercy on their souls." She moves her hands in a shooing motion and says, "Now, go with God and hurry."

The donkeys are unhappy about being rousted from their warm night beds and are braying loudly. Their noise makes the horse jittery.

We all embrace the nuns who have come out to see us off. We know we are unlikely to ever see them again. When I come to Æbba, I hold her close and whisper, "Thank you, mother, for all your generosities toward me and my travelling companions. I will send word of our fate when I am able."

The stable lad cups his hands and gives the women a lift onto the backs of the donkeys and Ovin mounts the horse. Our sad and frightened little band trots off into the night.

Some hours later, as we jostle along the forest track in silence, I busy myself thanking God that after Bishop Chad died at Litchfield in the year of our Lord 672, Ovin came north again and joined the brothers at Coldingham.

This perilous journey would be unthinkable without him by my side.

There is someone else I should give thanks to God for, but I do not know who it is. I think about who would have sent the messenger bird to warn us. Only the pigeon master and his apprentice have access to the birds who are kept in luxury within the castle walls. I decide it must have been the young lad. I remember I helped his sister a few winters ago when she had a baby in her belly and no husband to provide for her. There was a man and his wife I knew who were desperate for a child. We came to a good arrangement for all. Yes, it must have been the young lad. But how would he know about Ecgfrith's plan? I remember he was friends with the stable lad. Perhaps he overheard the nobles talking amongst themselves while they readied their mounts, and he told the bird boy. I decide to thank God for both these boys and ask him to hold them in his love.

We are riding away to the south from Coldingham, and not one of my companions has asked me where we are going. Their blind loyalty humbles me. After the third hour of riding, we decide to rest both ourselves and our animals by a little creek. The water is clear and sweet and each of us drinks heartily from our cupped hands. Then we all melt into the forest for a few minutes to relieve our bladders.

When everyone is back in our little clearing, I say, "Whatever happens on this perilous journey, your loyalty and your willingness to give up the safety of the monastery for me will never be forgotten. I promise you, if we are spared, I will reward you while you still live and our Lord will reward you when you achieve your heavenly peace. Now, I believe our best chance is to make for my island of Eels in East Anglia where we will be beyond Ecgfrith's reach unless his determination is entirely crazed. It is homeland to all of us, and we will be able to begin our new lives there in safety. In the next few days, we will arrive at Hild's monastery. We will rest and replenish our provisions there."

Ovin speaks up. "Forgive me, dear sister, but I do not believe it is wise to go to Hild, though I know how desperately you wish to. It is the first place King Ecgfrith will look for us when he learns that you have fled from Coldingham. He will surely order soldiers to guard the Whitby Road."

In my heart, I know he is right but the disappointment is so bitter in my throat, I cannot speak. I nod reluctant agreement with his wisdom. After giving each of us women a hand up on our own donkey, he mounts the horse. We start off again along the forest track, shivering miserably and fearful of the night animals and other wild things that may be watching us as we pass.

Our journey is now leading us through open country along the seacoast. We are walking the animals to rest them when, underneath our feet, we begin to feel the dreaded hoofbeats of Ecgfrith's warhorses pounding the hard ground.

"They are too close, my lady," warns Ovin. "We cannot escape them on these poor animals."

Then Freyda, who is up ahead, shouts back to us. "There is a large rock out to sea a little farther along. The tidewater is beginning to rise but, if we hurry, we may be able to make the rock in time and hide behind it."

We all push on more quickly. It is a desperate move to go to the rock, but we seem to have little other choice. By the time we reach the shore and the big stone some way out, the tide has risen by three hands. We slog through the water, fighting the power of the sea to pull us under. When we reach the rock, we all clamber up as best we can, searching for little handholds to grip and pulling the animals up behind us.

Looking around, we realize we are on a small island with just enough land surrounding the stone to give the animals and ourselves some standing room. The rock, we quickly discover, is not large enough to conceal all of us. It is too late to hide in any event because Ecgfrith and his nobles have pounded up to the spit of mainland opposite the rock and we are entirely exposed to the shore.

The tide is full now, and they will not risk their warhorses to come and get us. As we huddle together against the rock, we realize how woefully inadequate is our sanctuary. It was a dreadful move to come out here but terror made us foolish.

Ecgfrith and his nobles glare angrily at us from the shore, but they can do no other than wait for the tide to ebb and then come and fetch us off the rock.

The nuns and I begin to pray heartily together for deliverance, and Freyda starts to moan woefully. I gather her under my cloak and think, in that desperate moment, that were I to perform this solitary act of compassion for a person beneath my dignity in my former life, tongues would be clucking, not only among the noble class but among the servants as well.

We continue to pray and the king and his warriors continue to glare.

With no warning, the sea suddenly blows up in an almighty storm. Waves crash all around us. The noise is horrifying. The fury of the sea rages ever stronger and stronger, soaking us all with salt spray. Our horse screams in panic, rearing up on his hind legs. I am terrified he will slide into the sea and be lost to us. Ovin is trying desperately to control and calm him. The little donkeys bray pitifully and huddle together on their small patch of land beside the rock.

Gradually, the menacing stares of the nobles turn to dread. We watch fearfully as these seasoned men of battle argue in terror amongst themselves and with Ecgfrith. Some of these soldiers were with Oswiu at the battle of the Winwæd, and they know only too well how an entire army can be crushed by a whim of nature. That day, a flash flood drowned most of the evil Penda's warriors. God worked for them at the Winwæd, but this time, they seem sore afraid he is against them.

After much shouting and angry gesturing, the nobles mount their terrified steeds and pull them away from the shore. Ecgfrith has not much choice but to follow. Our little band is left alone in what threatens to become a watery grave.

Black nights follow pale days and still the breakers beat against the rock. There is no difference between high tide and low. Our hairs and skins are coated with salt and our coarse wool habits are soaked and heavy. We have made a certain place behind the rock to relieve ourselves in some privacy but after several days with no water or food, we seldom require it. The rock moss and seaweeds that wash up are briny and make the animals vomit when they eat it. We cup what little water our bodies produce in our hands as it dribbles out of us, but what little we are able to drink we soon retch up again. I begin to believe our thirst will drive us mad. All seems lost as we are in failing health and beginning to see spectres and nightmarish visions. We barely have strength to pray together.

But God in his mercy hears the silent prayers of our hearts, and on about the fourth or fifth day, a spring of fresh water miraculously spurts from the rock. We grasp at the water with cupped hands and suck it into our parched and ragged throats. Ovin warns us to take only a little at a time at first lest we become ill. This is a miracle from the blessed heart of our loving and merciful God. As soon as we are able to speak, we offer up prayers of grateful thanksgiving. We attempt to sing our hallelujahs, but we are too weak to hear ourselves above the storm.

By the sixth or seventh day, I know not which, the winds gradually lessen and the sea begins to calm itself. Our little group continues to drink from the sacred spring and sing praises to Almighty God for driving away our persecutors and miraculously saving us from capture.[101]

When the tide at last recedes, we lead our severely weakened animals off the great stone island toward the mainland. As soon as we gain the shore, I dig into the fold in my salt stiffened habit and find my oilskin packet. Miraculously, all is still dry inside the bag.

We find a small river of good water and allow the animals to pasture and rest for two days. Delay is dangerous, but we must wait patiently until the beasts are stronger. Unbundling the extra garments that Æbba gave us, we spread them out on the ground to dry. We see then that she has taken them from the storeroom where the clothes are kept that the nuns and brothers discarded when they took the habit.

We spend the days foraging for berries and herbs for ourselves amongst the ground stubble and the shore bushes. Ovin manages to spear a goodly fish which we attempt to bake on a sunny rock as all the wood around us is too wet from the storm for a fire. It is mostly raw when we eat it but it feels like a feast to us. When the clothes are dry, we change into them and spread our religious garments. As soon as they have dried, we shake the salt from them and fold them into bundles for the donkeys to carry. We will have to wash everything properly when we come to another fresh stream on our travels.

Fearing that Ecgfrith will decide to return for me, we continue our flight on the second night after the storm.

After several days have passed, we arrive at the great Humber. Ovin finds a man with a sound boat to take us across a little to the east of the Ermine Street[102] crossing as we still fear that Ecgfrith will have posted guards.

Even as we travel through the forests of Elmet and Lindsay, our little band does not feel safe since this country had been, until recently, a holding of Ecgfrith's. We believe it possible that some men still loyal to him might discover our identity and take us, hoping for rewards and Ecgfrith's good favour. As we travel through the thick forests, the memory of Hild's tale of outlaws from her first feast with us at Rendlesham is ever in my mind.

In one of the villages, we learn that Wulfhere, King of Mercia and husband to my niece, Ermenilda, is now over king in Lindsay. I reckon I might be able to appeal to him on grounds of kinship if we are captured. This does little to allay our fears as we all know this forest abounds with outlaws who care little for kinship ties, having forfeited their own, and who would slaughter us for our few meagre possessions. Some people still believe the forest is home to wildlings who are enslaved by the dark arts and who practise human sacrifice to the old gods.

Still disguised as pilgrims, we seek out small settlements where the peasants know only their work on the land and nought of the plots and schemes of the nobility. We encounter much dangerous suspicion as we pass through settlements where villagers live in squalid huts that they share with their animals and where strangers seldom come by. Ovin says they might think we are outlaws in disguise. I point out that it would be a peculiar band of outlaws that is made up of one old man and four women.

When we come to the settlement of Stow in Lindsay, we are particularly well met and decide to rest there awhile as we are all strained to our very limits. Weariness overcomes me, and I thrust my walking stick into the earth and fall to the ground. I am asleep before I have finished my prayers.

When I feel the dawn light on my eyes, I awaken and am astonished to see that overnight my walking stick has sprung buds and leaves. I waken the others and we all fall to our knees in gratitude for this sign that God's loving mercy is still with us.

When they witness this miracle, the villagers, who have previously been taught to know God, fall to their knees in praise of our Lord and in honour of us. A feast is given, such as they are able to provide. There is good ale and dancing and singing into the next night. Although as nuns we have forsaken this kind of behaviour, we find ourselves entering into it with joyful hearts in thanks to God for this precious sign of his love. The next day, the villagers hurriedly craft me a new staff so that the miracle may remain growing in their settlement.[103]

As we prepare to leave, many small trinkets are pressed into our hands to ensure continued safe passage on our journey. Although we believe only in God's mercy for our safety, we happily accept these tokens of our new friends' wishes for us.

At last after many strenuous and terrifying weeks of travel, we cross into our homeland of East Anglia. We fall to the ground, pressing our faces into the sacred earth of our ancestors and offering up praises to God. We are all so prostrate and weary that much time passes before we are able to carry on. Knowing we are safe at last, we don our religious clothing once again.

Eventually, we arrive in my own land, the Island of Eels, that my dear Tondberht had bestowed on me many years ago. Weeping with relief and joy, I separate myself from the others and enter the little church I had built there before I went north to marry Ecgfrith. Dropping to my knees, I lay prone on the old stone floor and pray well into the night in thanks to God for our deliverance.

When at last I emerge from my solitude, all are still riotously dancing and singing. I weep again in gratitude for this joyful welcome from my beloved people who I had been compelled by fortune to leave twelve winters ago.

THE COVENANT FULFILLED

The Island of Eels, East Anglia, Britain

Being comprised of letters between Hild and Etheldreda

During the years of our Lord 674 and 679

Letter Fourteen

Summer in the year of our Lord 674
To Hild, Abbess of Whitby
From Etheldreda, Abbess of Ely

My beloved friend, Hild,
Between my last letter and this has occurred two years of unimaginable wonders. I truly believe that God, in his infinite mercy, has gathered this humble servant into his bosom of bountiful love. I believe I have been given the task of illuminating his endless compassion, wisdom, and love to his people in this corner of Britain where I first began my life. How else to explain the miracles I have experienced?

Sadly, my supply of parchment has dwindled to only a few skins, so I will be unable to relate my astounding adventures in their entirety to you at this time. Perhaps when I am better established here, I will be able to secure some more material and I will then write the whole wondrous story to you. As you can see, I have been forced to scrape one of your beloved letters in order to write this one to you. For now, I will tell you only that I was forced to flee Northumbria and have arrived safely in my own land on the Island of Eels.

As soon as it was possible, I made it known that I intended to build a monastery near Ely where men and women could enter religious life and where the children of the land, and even grown folk who wished it, could be made to read and write. Wishing to help improve the lives of their countrymen, strong men from all around came and worked on the buildings until they were done. They erected the buildings on a hill above the low surrounding fen-land. The nave of the church has windows ornamented with pillars and arches, and the choir is arched with stone. Ealdwulf, kin to us both and now king of East Anglia,[104] provided some materials and workers.

I have a separate apartment from which I can enter the church privately. We have a dormitory for the nuns and a separate building with a parlour for the reception of strangers. The dormitory for the men is over the parlour.[105] The women of the countryside assumed the farm chores while the men were working and, sooner than I might have imagined, my monastery was a real thing and I was a genuine abbess.[106] Wonder of wonders!

I have had another piece of news that may be of interest to you. King Cenwalh, who you knew at Rendlesham, passed into the heavenly kingdom two years ago and his wife, the one he discarded Penda's sister for, ruled on her own for one year as the first ever queen of Wessex.[107] What do you think of that?

I have only a little more space in which to write. Although it sorely grieves my heart, I fear I will have to scrape the rest of your letters in order to have writing materials for my school. I know you will understand the importance of this, but I count it a grievous personal loss as, in times of stress,

I have taken to rereading your letters as a source of comfort and inspiration. They have travelled safely with me from East Anglia to Northumbria and back to East Anglia only to be destroyed, out of necessity, by my own hand.

Be happy for me, dear Mother, as my every dream has been realized and given to me by our most merciful and loving God.

Etheldreda, Abbess of Ely
(I weep with joy as I write abbess next to my name.)

Letter Fifteen

Spring in the year of our Lord 675
To Etheldreda, Abbess of Ely
From Hild, Abbess of Whitby

My dear child, if I may still address you so, I was overjoyed to receive your last missive. After learning that you had been released from court to take holy orders at Coldingham, I wrote a letter to you there, exhilarating in your newfound joy. In reply, Abbess Æbba sent me a short missive by travellers explaining your hasty departure. That was three years past. During that time, having no news from you, I heartily feared for your fate. I have always believed that our dear Lord has cradled you from birth in the palm of his hand, but in times of personal darkness when the demons come, I have sometimes questioned that belief. I thank God to know that you are safe in your homeland and that you have achieved your life-long desire to live the peaceful and challenging life of an abbess. I imagine by now that your numbers have grown and that your community is thriving under your care.

Some months ago, I had the most felicitous visit from an old and venerated friend, Benedict Biscop. I am certain you will have heard of his many journeys to Rome to visit the tombs of the Apostles and to be instructed in the mysteries of the faith. As a young man and being of noble birth, he was a favoured thane at King Oswiu's court (long before your time), but when he was twenty-five years old, he renounced the secular world to seek a place in religious life. On his first journey to Rome, he was accompanied by his good friend, Wilfrid (yes, that Wilfrid), but they were separated when Wilfrid remained at Lyons.

When Biscop returned this time to his homeland, Ecgfrith gave him land at Wearmouth to build a monastery dedicated to that most holy of Apostles, Peter, the rock on which Christ himself built his church. My own eyes have not seen it, but he told me that it is built of stone by men brought across the sea from Francia because no one in Northumbria remembered that skill they had learned from the Romans. It even has glazed windows to keep out the elements. He believes they are the first in Britain. Benedict collected many books and relics and adornments for his new church, some of which he brought with him to Whitby as gifts for our monastery.[108] *I straightaway set my scribes to the task of copying these books so that I may in turn share them with other communities.*[109] *I am hoping that some will be able to find their way to you, but I shall have to seek out a trusted emissary for such an important task. When Benedict left to return to his work at Wearmouth, my spirit was uplifted, and I was convinced that his visit had been one of the mysterious ways in which God works because his visit came at a time in my life when I have been sorely tried by physical ailment.*

Since two winters past, I have been afflicted by a great fever and a violent heat within my body. I have continued publicly to instruct my flock in the virtue of praising God and giving thanks both in adversity of health and in well-being,[110] but I confess in the dark, small hours before dawn, I am beset by demons of the worst nature, and I pray, just as Christ did, to our loving Lord to take this cup from me.[111] I would welcome the heavenly kingdom, but I feel in my heart, though I have achieved a life of sixty-one winters, my work is not yet done in the earthly realm.

Pray for me, dear Dreda, as I have prayed for you all these many years. Pray that God will spare me a few more winters to continue to work in his kingdom on earth.

Hild, Abbess of Whitby

Letter Sixteen

Autumn in the year of our Lord 676
To Hild, my mother in Christ and Abbess of Whitby
From Etheldreda, Abbess of Ely

My dear Hild,

I am heartbroken to learn that you are in ill health. My prayers for your healing and those of all in my community wing their way towards our Lord at every office of each day. Please know, dear mother, that we are holding you in our hearts in the certain knowledge that God's will regarding you, his beloved servant, will be accomplished in his good time.

My dear sister, Seaxburga, and her daughter, Ermenilda, have joined our community at Ely. I am overjoyed by this reconciliation. You will remember when you and I first met those long years ago how sorrowful I was that Seaxburga had been sent to Kent to marry King Eorconberht. I mentioned that her husband died of plague some while ago, and she has since been at her own monastery in Sheppey. And now Ermenilda is a widow, as her husband, the great Wulfhere, has died not too many months ago. Ermenilda went to her mother at Sheppey and together, they decided to travel here to Ely and make their home in our community.

When I had news of their coming, I wondered how it would be between us because only two years ago, Ecgfrith launched a great battle against Wulfhere for control of Mercia, and Wulfhere was defeated. He did not die in the battle but succumbed to disease the following year. I decided to discuss this with my sister and my niece when they arrived, so that it would not stand between us and impede our work here. Both assured me that, since women have little power over what men do and that, since temporal matters and matters of the spirit are quite separate, there would be no cause for unsettled feelings.

Apart from your own illness, there is another shadow over my joy in my present life. My beloved Ovin passed to his heavenly reward one winter past at nearly the same time as Wulfhere. Never has anyone had such a loyal and devoted friend as that dear man was to me. I am sure in my heart that were it not for him, we would never have survived our flight from Coldingham and arrived safely in Ely to begin our great work here. We were all in the hands of God, but Ovin was his blessed instrument on earth.

I miss him terribly, but I thank God that I had such a friend during our time on earth together. I have caused to be erected a stone monument in his memory and placed it on a hillside near his church in his own village of Haddenham, where he was greatly loved and respected. The inscription reads, "Give, O God, to Ovin, Thy Light and Rest. Amen."[112] *I shall never forget his service to me, and my nuns and I pray every day for his soul.*

Life here at Ely is simple and spare. In thanks to our Lord for our safe arrival here, I have made it my habit to wear rough woollen garments and take hot baths only before the great Christian festivals of Easter, Whitsuntide, and Epiphany. But first my assistants and I help to wash all the other nuns in the monastery. It is my fervent wish to be a true servant of the servants of God. I take no more than one meal each day and spend several hours in prayer as each blessed new day dawns.[113]

Much of the time that I spend in prayer, I am praying for you, my dear friend, that you will be relieved of your fever and that Christ will lay his healing hands upon you and you will be whole again. It is the dearest wish of my heart.

We are sorely lacking in books and materials for learning here at Ely. If it is God's will that copies of some of Benedict's books find their way to our community, many humble prayers of thanksgiving will be lifted up to heaven.

*Your daughter in Christ,
Etheldreda, Abbess of Ely*

Letter Seventeen

Spring in the year of our Lord 677
To Etheldreda, Abbess of Ely
From Hild, Abbess of Whitby

My dear, dear Dreda,

How happy I am for you that you have been reunited with your beloved sister and niece. I think of the joy this brings into your life and my heart swells. It has always been a source of great sadness to me that I have never again seen my sister, Hereswitha. I know from a letter I received a few winters ago that she has found happiness in her life at Chelles, and that is as much as we can hope for those we love.

I have received news that Bishop Colman, who you will remember from the great gathering, entered into his heavenly life last year after many years of service to the church in Scotland and Ireland. Even after Oswiu's decision for the Roman tradition, Colman continued to preach the Celtic ways and accomplished many good works, converting souls to the true faith and founding new church communities.

There will be good news for you on the arrival of this missive, as it is accompanied by three books that my scribes have copied for your community at Ely. They are 'Confessions', 'On Christian Doctrine', and 'On the Trinity', all from the unequalled mind and hand of St. Augustine of Hippo.[114] *They will give your community much to study and discuss, and they will, without fail, instil in all of us a deeper and clearer understanding of our relationship with God. I wish you much joy in them.*

The rigorous life you have described for yourself does not seem to allow for much pleasure or laughter. Even the Rule of Benedict of Nursia does not call for measures so severe.[115] *I think, my child, that God does not demand such strictures on our part to prove our love for him. He knows what is in our hearts and will love us always. Although I believe this with my whole being, I am also troubled by this belief. As you know, after all these years, I have been unable to relieve myself of feelings of ill will toward my old nemesis, the odious Wilfrid. Indeed, rumours abound that I have allied myself with Archbishop Theodore and other significant leaders of the Northumbrian church against Wilfrid.*[116] *He has made many powerful enemies in the north and is unlikely to come to a good end.*

Still I fear that, even though to my mind and heart Wilfrid is worthy of such enmity, God would wish me to find forgiveness for him within my own being before I leave this earthly realm.

My fever still rages, and I become more feeble with each passing winter. Even Ælfflæd with her exceptional powers of healing has been unable to give me relief. I sometimes wonder if this is our beloved Lord working within me to burn out my hatred of Wilfrid and purify my heart and mind. If so, I believe he must find another way because this one is not working. The very name of Wilfrid only serves to add fuel to the fire within me. I pray every day that, when I enter the heavenly kingdom, the work I have done for our Lord on earth and the life that I have dedicated to him will be sufficient to overcome the burden of hostility I still bear toward Wilfrid, who is, after all, also a dedicated worker for God's church. I suppose he is not to blame for his detestable and vainglorious nature, but still I cannot abide him. God forgive me and have mercy upon my soul when, at the last day, I stand before him.

Until we meet again, Dreda, I remain your loving friend, and I continue to fervently praise God for his blessing of our abiding devotion and loving care of each other throughout the many winters since he first saw fit for us to come into each other's lives.

Your loving mother in Christ, Hild

Letter Eighteen

Spring in the Year of our Lord, 679
To Hild, Abbess of Whitby
From Etheldreda, Abbess of Ely

Oh, my dear mother Hild,

You will see immediately that this missive is not in my hand. Being too weak myself, I have asked Freyda to write for me as she has learned her letters and has just last month made her vows.

The exciting news is that I have been blessed with a vision for my passing to the heavenly realm.[117] *Soon, all the cares of this world will be behind me, and I will bask in the splendour of our Lord's light. Since making this known to my community, many wander about here with mournful faces. Freyda is one of the worst offenders. I have instructed all of my flock to be joyful that I will soon be with our Lord and his beloved Son. Without meaning to sound prideful, their gloomy countenances bespeak their feelings of loss for my earthly person and my loving guidance in the religious life.*

The books of St. Augustine that you have sent to us have been a great boon. I have had them read and reread to me, as I am too weak to hold them, and studied each of them to the detriment of my time for prayers. I have been so profoundly enlightened by them that I see the hand of God in their arrival while I still have time to plumb the depths of their wisdom and knowledge of our Christian belief. I have instructed my nuns and the brethren to study these books assiduously after I am gone that they may better understand the mind of our God and the workings of our church.

Were you able to see the wondrous star comet that raced through the heavens for three months last year?[118] *It surely was a sign from God to his earthly creations of his ever-abiding love and presence.*

When I am gone from the earth, Seaxburga will become abbess. I know that she will continue with grace and dignity the work I have begun here. She is already beloved by my flock and will have no difficulty in assuming the rule of the monastery.

For some time now I have been suffering from the pain afforded me by a large swelling under my jaw. I have taken no food for several days because it is too difficult to swallow. I do take some small sips of warm ale when my thirst is unbearable. I suffer this affliction with gratitude because I believe God in his goodness has sent it to me to absolve me from the guilt of too much pleasure in wearing jewels about my neck when I younger. The healer, Cynefrith, came and opened the swelling to let out the noxious matter and the relief has given me the strength to say these final words to you.[119]

I give you my blessing, my beloved friend, to scrape the remainder of my letters so that your scholars will have material with which to work. With great reluctance, I have done the same to the remaining ones of yours.

Do not be disheartened. When I think of my body washed clean of all the sins and grime of this world and anointed with herbs and spices and wrapped in fresh clean linen in preparation for my journey to God, I am overcome with rapture. Sometimes I am surrounded by angels whose singing is so wondrous that it transports me to a place where my body has no weight and I feel no pain. It will not be long now before I begin my journey. I will wait for you in the heavenly kingdom, my dearest friend, and all the cares of this sorry world will be but a fading memory as we live anew in the reflection of our Lord's glory for all eternity.

Your loving daughter in Christ,
Etheldreda

APPENDIX

After the year of our Lord 679

St. Hild of Whitby

Hild survived her great friend, Etheldreda, by only one year, succumbing to her fever at the age of 66 on November 17 in the year of our Lord 680 after six years of illness. Events surrounding her death have become the stuff of legend. In *HE*, Bede reports two miracles. The first took place in a monastery thirteen miles distant from Whitby, where a nun, awakened by the sound of the bell that marked a death in the monastery, opened her eyes and saw the top of the house open, a great light shine in, and the soul of Hild attended and conducted to heaven by angels. Another report came from a nun in Hild's own monastery, who was passing the night in the remotest part of the monastery with a group of newly converted women. She, too, in the very same hour as Hild's death, reported seeing Hild's soul ascend to heaven in the company of angels.[120]

St. Etheldreda of Ely

Etheldreda died June 23 in the year of our Lord 679 at the age of forty-nine years. It is unknown whether her demise was from plague or tumour. As she had ordered, she was buried amongst her flock in a plain wooden coffin. Sixteen years later, her sister Seaxburga decided her bones should be translated to a white marble coffin and buried within the church walls. When her previous coffin was opened, all in attendance marvelled to see that Etheldreda's body was as fresh as the day it had first been buried. Cynefrith, her physician, was astounded to see that the great gaping wound on her neck that had been present when she died was merely a tiny scar. Her priest, Huna, who had celebrated the funeral of the Holy Mother also presided at her translation. At this time in the history of the church, a body that had been buried and exhumed many years later and found to be uncorrupted was cause for sainthood to be conferred upon the deceased. Etheldreda became variously known as St. Æthelthryth and St. Audrey.[121]

The Monk of Ely was much taken with Etheldreda and called her a "dulcifluous mother" *(LE*, 1:7) to her flock and states that while growing up, she was always "pleasant, sweet, and gentle to everybody" and "pious, saintly, and devout from an early age." (*LE*, 1:16) He also claims, on the basis of written evidence, that Etheldreda in her lifetime "cured the lame, gave sight also to the blind, and healed innumerable people in the name of Jesus." (*LE*, 1: 37)

Ecgfrith, King of Northumbria 670-685

Although Etheldreda seems to have had little regard or respect for her boy-husband, Bede speaks glowingly of his devoutness and his nobility of mind and action. (*HE*, IV:xix) During his fifteen-year reign, Northumbria was enjoying the most powerful time in its history. However, Ecgfrith's private life was full of contentious issues. He had been burdened with a queen who refused to consummate the marriage, thereby making him a source of ridicule among his nobles.

As mentioned previously, he asked Bishop Wilfrid (the same priest who spoke at the Synod of Whitby) to try to persuade Etheldreda that the kingdom needed an heir. Wilfrid accepted a great deal of money and land in order to accomplish this and, in the end, persuaded the king to let Etheldreda retire to a monastery. Naturally, bitter feelings between Ecgfrith and Wilfrid abounded and destroyed their already tentative relationship.

By 672, Ecgfrith's marriage to Etheldreda had been dissolved, and he married his longtime mistress, Eormenburg.

Ecgfrith's military accomplishments included defeating the Picts in Scotland in 672 and Wulfhere of Mercia who was trying to reclaim Lindsay in 674. He was in turn defeated by Æthelred, Wulfhere's successor, at the River Trent in 679. He then won a victory in Ireland in 684, which earned him the wrath of Bede, who was incensed by the carnage to which that innocent nation was subjected.

The next year, he again attacked the Picts, but his troops were ambushed at Nechtansmere near Forfar in Scotland, where Ecgfrith was killed on May 20, 685. Having completely revised his opinion of Ecgfrith, Bede as much as claims his demise was his own fault because he did not listen to the advice of his friends, nobles, and Cuthbert, recently appointed Bishop of Lindisfarne, who all tried to dissuade him from this campaign. (*HE*, IV:xxvi) Ecgfrith's queen, Eormenburg, retired to obscurity in Carlisle Abbey.

Saint Wilfrid c. 634-709

Much has been written regarding Wilfrid's tumultuous career in religion and in politics which, in the early centuries of the Christian church, were much the same thing. His life abounds with paradoxes. To some he was a great hero of the church, and to others, he was an annoyance that just wouldn't go away. He amassed a very large fortune and delighted in the rich religious garments of pomp and ceremony in public, yet in private, he lived a simple ascetic life.

His quarrelsome personality engendered many enemies among the rich and powerful, yet he charmed many others with his good looks, piety, erudition, and devotion. He claimed to be the first to introduce the monastic rule of St. Benedict of Nursia to Britain. He is considered to be one of the greatest missionaries of the early church and one of the strongest of the Anglo-Saxon saints.

Whenever he felt his rights and privileges as a bishop were being trampled upon, he scurried off to Rome to put his case to the highest authorities. These journeys meant he was away from Britain for years at a time, as he was wont to stay for months in European courts where he felt more appreciated and where he found the opportunity for evangelizing.

Hild was never able to forgive Wilfrid for his humiliation of Colman, Bishop of Lindisfarne, at the Synod of Whitby and was rumoured to be involved in several conspiracies against him with other powerful religious figures of the time. Etheldreda, on the other hand, was eternally grateful to him for convincing Ecgfrith to free her from their marriage. Later, he earned the enmity of Eormenburg, Ecgfrith's second wife, and paid the price of banishment from Northumbria. He was allowed to return when Alchfrith became king upon Ecgfrith's death.

Wilfrid left his unhappy childhood home at an early age and joined Oswiu's court after deciding to devote his life to the church. With Queen Eanflæd's help, he began his career studying first at Lindisfarne, where he learned the Irish traditions, and then in Kent, where he was educated in the Roman way. He was so impressed by Rome that he abandoned any lingering love for the Irish church and fully embraced the Roman church. After a long and varied career in which he accomplished much to expand the emergent Christian church in Britain, he suffered a series of strokes and succumbed to these afflictions on April 24, 709.[122] He was buried at Ripon.[123]

St. Æbba of Coldingham

Sadly, Æbba's reputation suffers from history remembering only one story about her life to the detriment of her many good works and her devotion to God's kingdom on earth. As mentioned earlier in the text, when Ecgfrith was finally persuaded to let Etheldreda go to a monastery, it was Æbba, Ecgfrith's aunt, who took Etheldreda in and schooled her in preparation for taking her vows. And it was Æbba who helped Etheldreda escape when Ecgfrith changed his mind and came after her.

Æbba was a friend of St. Cuthbert and a trusted advisor to many noble and royal visitors. But the most infamous legend connected to her involves the unseemly behaviour of the nuns and monks under her care.[124] For whatever reason, discipline could not be maintained at Coldingham and charges of wearing fine garments, feasting, and lax sexual mores were levelled against the monastery. It was predicted that a fire would be sent from heaven and consume Coldingham after Æbba's death. According to the Anglo-Saxon Chronicle, that is exactly what happened in 679, the same year as Etheldreda's death. Zealots of the day, including Bede, were convinced it was God's vengeance on the too worldly lifestyle of the inmates of

Coldingham. Thus, the considerable amount of good that Æbba did was consigned to the shadows. The tales of misbehaviour by those in her charge captured the light.

Eanflæd and Ælfflæd

Following Hild's death in 680, Eanflæd, former wife of King Oswiu of Northumbria, and her daughter, Ælfflæd, jointly ruled the double monastery that Hild had founded at Whitby. When Eanflæd died sometime after 685, Ælfflæd became the sole abbess of Whitby and remained so until her death in 714.

Having lived all of her life in the monastery at Whitby where the nuns practised medicine, Ælfflæd was well known for her surgical skills and her personal attention to her patients. She was a familiar of the venerated St. Cuthbert of Lindisfarne. A miracle is attributed to Cuthbert regarding Ælfflæd. In his chapters on Cuthbert, Bede attests to her being afflicted with a terrible life-threatening illness unknown to the physicians. By Divine Grace, she is said to have been saved from death but left unable to walk or stand. She wished for Cuthbert to send her a possession of his that she might be cured. A linen girdle was sent from him, and after putting it on, Ælfflæd was able to stand and in three days was perfectly cured.[125]

Ælfflæd was praised throughout her life for her holiness, devotion, and counselling skills, both in the personal and the political spheres of her time. When she died, she was buried at Whitby beside her parents, King Oswiu and Queen Eanflæd, and her grandfather, the sainted King Edwin.

Endnote Abbreviations for Frequently Cited Sources

ASC — *Anglo-Saxon Chronicle*

BE — *The Blackwell Encyclopaedia of Anglo-Saxon England*

CE — *The Conversion of the English*

DR — *Douay-Rheims New Testament Bible*

EP — *Etheldreda, Princess, Queen, Abbess & Saint*

HE — *Historia ecclesiastica gentis Anglorum*
(Ecclesiastical History of the English Church and People)

LE — *Liber Eliensis (The Book of Ely)*

MWM — *Medieval Women Monastics*

WM — *Women under Monasticism*

Endnotes

1. After occupying Britain for the best part of five hundred years, the legions were recalled to Rome to defend against marauding barbarian hordes of Goths, Vandals, and Huns from the east who began moving west across Europe early in the fifth century.

2. Tradition has it that two brothers, Hengest and Horsa, were invited to Britain by a "tyrant" named Vortigern. They were among the first Anglo-Saxon invaders to establish kingdoms for themselves after revolting against the rule of Vortigern. They were particularly associated with the area that became known as Kent. Hengest is considered the founder of the Kentish royal dynasty. Bede offers his version of these events in the *History of the English Church and People*. I: xii and xv, hereafter identified as *HE*.

3. Simon Keynes, "Heptarchy", *The Blackwell Encyclopaedia of Anglo-Saxon England* eds. Michael Lapidge et al. (Oxford: Blackwell, 1999), 233, hereafter identified as *BE*.

4. For a more detailed account of feuds, the process by which one kinship group could legally exact revenge on another group that had dishonoured it in some manner, and wergild, the amount of money set by law on the value of different members of Anglo-Saxon society, see Kennedy, *BE*, 182–83 and Hough, *BE*, 469–70.

5. Dorothy Whitelock notes that if a convicted member does not pay his fine and if his kindred also fails to pay the fines and compensations, he becomes an outlaw and "anyone could kill him with impunity, and anyone who harboured him, or, worse still, took vengeance for his slaying, became liable to very heavy penalties. The outlaw could recover his rights only by a king's pardon" [Dorothy Whitelock, *The Beginnings of English Society* (Middlesex, England: Penguin, 1952), 140].

6. Bretwalda, a term used to signify "ruler of Britain", was intended to denote supremacy over all the sub-kings and people who lived south of the Humber River. It is likely to have been more of a nominal or honorary title than a real one. The term may not have come into use until the 9th century although Bede lists the seven kings to whom he attributes sovereignty or imperium over Britain in *HE,* II: v, a manuscript that made its original appearance around the year 733. The fifth, sixth, and seventh Bretwaldas — Edwin, Oswald, and Oswiu — were all Northumbrian kings whose political and military influence extended south of the Humber. (Keynes, *BE*, 74)

7. Kelly, *BE*, 13

8. For a general discussion of heathenism among the Anglo-Saxons, see Frank Stenton, *Anglo-Saxon England*, 3rd Ed. (Oxford: Oxford University Press, 1971), 96–102.

9. Archeological evidence supports the idea that there had been Christians in Britain in Roman times [G.R. Evans, *Faith in the Medieval World* (Downer's Grove, Il: Inter Varsity Press, 2002), 14.]

10. *The Catholic Encyclopedia* contains detailed biographies of each of these men under the headings of St. Augustine of Canterbury and St. Columba.

11. Computus, the medieval science of computation which was mostly concerned with the liturgical calendar and particularly with the setting of the dates of the moveable Christian feasts, is discussed more fully by Peter Baker (*BE*, 119–120).

12. Norman Sneesby, *Etheldreda Princess, Queen, Abbess & Saint* (Ely: Fern House, 1999), 14–15, hereafter identified as *EP*.

13. *The Anglo-Saxon Chronicle.* Trans. G.N. Garmonsway, (London: J.M. Dent, 1955), 34–35, 38–39, hereafter identified as *ASC*.

14. The "great hall" was the most important structure in Anglo-Saxon settlements. Commercial transactions took place there, justice was dispensed within its walls, disputes were settled, and

feasting and socializing were enjoyed. In the case of a royal hall, housing was provided for the lord and his family and, occasionally, worthy guests. Halls were almost always rectangular and varied considerably in size. A royal hall might be forty-five by eighty feet with small private chambers along the side, while an ordinary settlement hall might be as small as eighteen by thirty feet. They were generally built with wooden boards standing on end side by side and joined at the top by timber crossbeams. Their roofs were usually thatched with an opening for smoke from the fire pit to escape.

15. Around the end of the 9th century, these men would be oath-men who had sworn allegiance to their lord or king. There is not much evidence of this in earlier Anglo-Saxon life. It is more likely that in the 7th century "the warrior's loyalty to his lord arose from the latter's generosity, not from any ceremonial pledge". (Wormald, *BE*, 338).

16. Hild's arrival in East Anglia is recorded by Bede in *HE*, IV: xxiii.

17. Much confusion surrounds Hereswitha's position in the East Anglian royal family. She was most certainly married into it, but several theories have been promoted as to who her actual husband was. The most probable is that her husband was Æthelric, brother of Anna, because Æthelric is named as Ealdwulf's father, and Bede states that Hereswitha was Ealdwulf's mother (*HE*, IV:xxiii). Ealdwulf (a.k.a. Aldwulf) was seen as a legitimate heir to the Wuffinga dynasty, becoming king c. 663–64 and dying after a very long reign in 713. (*BE*, 509)

18. At this time, there were no existing religious houses for women in Britain. Therefore, most women wishing to enter religious life resorted to crossing the channel to the land of the Franks where the original model of the double house, monks and nuns living strictly separately under one abbess, had been already established.

19. Bede tells us that Coinwalch (Cenwalh) put aside his wife who was Penda's sister and married another, thereby incurring the wrath of Penda, king of the Mercians, who drove Cehwalh

out of Wessex. Cenwalh was not Christian when he arrived in East Anglia, but after some time in that Christian kingdom, he willingly embraced the faith (*HE*, III: vii).

20. Until the time of King Anna, East Anglia had had a checkered history of Christian conversion and pagan recidivism (*HE*, II: xv).

21. The vastly outnumbered and outpowered East Anglians under the rule of King Ecgric were forced into battle c. 635–40 by Penda of Mercia. Hoping to keep his troops from abandoning the field, King Ecgric brought the former king, Sigeberht, who had "once been a notable and a brave commander" before retiring to monastic life, to the battlefield. Sigeberht refused to arm himself and was cut down almost immediately. Ecgric and many of his warrior lords were killed soon after. As a result of this battle, Anna, a descendant of Wuffa, became king of East Anglia, under Mercian oversight. (*HE*, III: xviii)

22. Christianity "was adopted by all the Anglo-Saxon royal houses in the course of the seventh century. Christianity was attractive to kings because of the respect they could command as Christ's representatives on earth. It carried the prestige of the late Roman empire and brought literacy and classical learning to the Anglo-Saxons, as well as new concepts such as Roman land law." (B.A.E. Yorke, *BE*, 271)

23. *Galdorcræft* is an ancient word for magic and *galdorsangs* are incantations.

24. See endnotes 4 and 5.

25. See Lapidge, *BE*, 359 for further information on Paulinus.

26. The canonical hour of terce is generally 9 a.m.

27. The Monk of Ely describes Anna as "an exalted king upon a throne" who "presented himself to his servants as their equal, to priests as a humble man and, to the people, as someone agreeable. He was a man of amazing devoutness to the worship of God, amazing solicitude for the building of churches, a strong

defender of his homeland, to whose protection all those who would not withstand ambush and enemy invasion took refuge." (*LE*, 1:21)

28. Wattle is a framework of wood and woven twigs, which is filled with daub, a mixture of mud, straw, and animal dung.

29. Sneesby, *EP*, pp. 2–3.

30. Bede tells of the school in *HE*, III:xviii.

31. Felix is variously reported to have died on March 8th, 647 or 648. Since the date is immaterial to Etheldreda's story, I have settled on 647.

32. Sneesby, *EP*, 16–18

33. *HE*, II: xvi

34. Bede tells us only that Hild spent the first thirty-three years of her life 'living most nobly in the secular habit." (*HE*, IV: xxiii) Nancy Bauer, O.S.B., in her essay on Hild in the book *Medieval Women Monastics,* hereafter *MWM*, includes the statement that "some historians suggest she had to have been married for the simple reason that women of that period did not remain single, and that the change in her life at age thirty-three was prompted by widowhood." (19)

35. Though Patrick (387–461 C.E.) began life as a Roman-Briton late in the fourth century, he was kidnapped at an early age by Irish pirates and taken to Ireland as a slave. After many years, he escaped and returned to Britannia. Later, he returned to Ireland, the land of the Druids, to preach and convert the Irish to Christianity. At first, he was met with much hostility and distrust, but eventually became the beloved patron saint, who is still celebrated today.

36. Columba (521–597 C.E.) was born in Ireland and preached there for many years. He became involved in a dispute, which led to a battle in which many men were killed. He was allowed to go into exile and chose the island of Iona, just off the coast of

present-day Scotland, for his refuge. There he vowed to save as many souls for Christianity as had been lost in the battle. Iona produced many religious fathers, some of whom travelled to Lindisfarne in northern Britain and began their proselytizing there. Columba, along with St. Patrick and St. Brigit (451–525 C.E.), are the three principal saints of Ireland.

37. The term ealdorman was "originally applied to high-ranking men, including some of royal birth or quasi-regal status, the basis of whose power and authority was independent of the king." (Stafford, *BE*, 152–53)

38. Lauds canonical hour is variously called Matins. Though it is performed at six a.m. it is considered to be the first hour of the day.

39. The East Anglian royal dynasty known as the Wuffingas, takes it family name from Wuffa, the grandfather of Raedwald (acc. 616, d. 627). Subsequent kings are "the followers of the wolf". (HE, II: xv)

40. Mother's Night was a pagan ritual absorbed into Christian traditions and celebrated on the eve of Christ's Mass Day. In *HE*, Bede includes a letter, dated the year of our Lord 601, from Pope Gregory to the abbot, Mellitus, with advice on how to handle the pagan celebrations of the Germanic tribes when he arrives in Britain. He is instructed to maintain the temples and sacred places of the pagans and transform them into places of Christian worship when the inhabitants of that area have been converted to the faith. Gregory evidently believes that conversion will be more enduring if the converts believe their ancestral traditions are being respected in the new religion and if the old ways are gradually replaced by Christian worship. (*HE*, I: xxx)

41. See note on time at the end of the introduction.

42. Many of the monasteries that began to spring up in Britain in the 7th and 8th centuries were styled after the French model of "double houses", so-called because both monks and nuns lived within the confines of the monastery but in strictly separate quarters. The

head of the monastery was invariably the abbess while only the monks or priests or visiting bishops were authorized to say the Mass and the sacraments. (Lapidge, *BE*, 320–22)

43. *HE,* IV: xxiii

44. For more detail on the dispute between Oswiu and Oswine and Bede's enthusiastic dissertation on the excellent character of Oswine, see *HE*, III: xiv.

45. For more information on the life of Aidan, Bishop of Lindisfarne, see *HE*, III: iii, v, xiv–xvii, xxvi.

46. *HE,* IV: xxiii

47. In *Monastic Life in Anglo-Saxon England c. 600–900,* Sarah Foot suggests that, rather than the rule of Benedict of Nursia, Hild more likely followed the Irish rule of sixth century Columba. This rule calls for six daily offices with services being held at midnight, in the early morning, at the third sixth and ninth hours and at nightfall. There would be only three psalms for the daytime offices so that work would not be disrupted for too long. At nightfall and midnight, there would be twelve psalms and twenty-four psalms would be said or sung in the early morning (196).

48. Gyrwe means "fen-dweller", hence the Gyrwas are the people of the fens.

49. In Anglo-Saxon law, the bridegroom was required to present a "morgengyfu" (morning gift) to his bride after the consummation of the marriage. Presumably, Tondberht and Etheldreda had a secret agreement that the gift would be presented and publicly accepted even though their marriage would never be consummated. One must hope that Etheldreda's somewhat indiscreet letter would never fall into unfriendly hands as the husband she appears to admire and, perhaps, even love would be humiliated if their platonic relationship were to become public knowledge. Sneesby offers much speculation regarding the marriage arrangement and Tondberht's acceptance of the terms. (*EP*, 32–34)

50. One hide is the amount of land sufficient for the support of a peasant and his household. (Rosamond Faith, *BE*, 238-39) Contrast the 1200 hides of the Gyrwas with the 30,000 hides of the land of the Mercians. Peter Hunter Blair notes that Hild bought the land of 10 households for the endowment of Whitby in *An Introduction to Anglo-Saxon England,* p. 148.

51. The Parker Chronicle (A) of the *ASC* records 654 as the year of King Anna's death while the Laud Chronicle (E) claims it was 653.

52. Sneesby alludes to treachery on the part of Æthelhere (*EP*, 35) but offers no credible source for this comment.

53. Bede reports that thirty of Penda's commanders, including Dreda's uncle, were lost in battle. Because the river Winwæd, where the battle was fought, was mightily swollen with great rains and had overflowed its banks, many of the casualties were drowned rather than killed by Oswiu's troops. (*HE*, III: xxiv)

54. The Monk of Ely states, "They were not one in body but one spirit in Christ and dissension and discord never came between them." (*LE*, 1:18)

55. The Parker Chronicle (A) of the *ASC* claims the Battle of Winwidfeld (Winwæd) took place in 655, while the Laud Chronicle (E) claims it was in 654. In the same year, the Parker states that five thousand, eight hundred and fifty years had passed away from the beginning of the world. Laud claims it was a mere five thousand, eight hundred. The perishing in battle of Penda and thirty of his kin and Æthelhere, the sub-king of East Anglia, and many other warlords, resulted in far-reaching change in Mercia and East Anglia.

56. Evans describes the vision of heaven of Augustine of Hippo as an intellectual place "whose pleasures would consist in conversation with one's companions about spiritual things, the contemplation of truth, beauty and goodness and, above all, the joy of gazing into the mind of God and meeting him personally in an exchange of mutual understanding which would raise

the creature as high as it was capable of reaching, in an eternal rapture" (20). Heaven was thought to be above the earth and hell below. One level of hell was the realm of the dead where Jesus is said to have descended after his crucifixion and before his resurrection. The other is the hell of the damned in which there is no hope. According to Augustine, heaven-minded medieval Christians of good conscience were allowed to take pleasure "in the contemplation of the sufferings of those in hell, for they will reflect on the extraordinary mercy of God in rescuing them from the fate which they also deserved as sinners." (*Faith in the Medieval World*, 23–24)

57. *HE*, III: xxiv

58. Author's note: In pre-Viking sources, Whitby was known as *Streanæshalch*. It was the most important royal monastery in Deira and the burial place of the royal house of Northumbria. (Blair, *BE*, 472) Out of consideration for the reader, *Streanæshalch* will be referred to in this text as Whitby, the name given to it later by the Danes.

59. After Penda was killed at the battle of the Winwæd in 655, Oswiu, King of the Northumbrians, ruled Mercia for three years. In that time, he set up Peada, Penda's son, as King of the Southern Mercians, a kingdom of 5,000 families. Peada accepted the faith but was betrayed by some treachery of his queen (Oswiu's daughter) and killed at Easter after less than a year as king. Northumbrian ealdormen ruled in Mercia until Wulfhere was made king in 658. (*HE*, III: xxiv)

60. See Sneesby (*EP*, 47–49) for a speculative discussion of Seaxburga's role in the events of Etheldreda's life at this time.

61. Etheldreda's own village, about a mile south of present-day Ely.

62. The monk of Ely states they were "married with multifarious splendour and diverse celebrating dances of joyous people." (*LE*, 1:26)

63. *HE*, IV: xxiii

64. Historically, this meeting which had profound implications for the fledgling church in Britain, is known as The Synod of Whitby. Many sources say the gathering of churchmen took place in 664, others suggest 663 and some make no claim regarding the date of the event.

65. Alchfrith was Oswiu's son by his first wife, Rieinmelth, who Oswiu married as a young man while in exile among the Scots of Dal Riada. (Holdsworth, *BE*, 349) Oswiu gave him the sub-kingship in Deira c. 655.

66. The Scots were also called Irish probably because St. Columba, the man responsible for the Christian conversion of the peoples of Northern Britain, sailed originally across the sea from Ireland to Iona in the Scots land.

67. As we shall learn in more detail later, the reason for the calling of the meeting of churchmen was to decide once and for all which tradition would be followed in Britain — the Irish (or Celtic), instituted by St. Columba in 563, or the Roman, brought to the southern part of Britain by St. Augustine in 597. Queen Eanflaed, being the daughter of Æthelburh and granddaughter of Æthelberht of Kent, was raised in the Roman tradition, while Oswiu was of the Irish persuasion.

68. Hadrian's Wall, begun in 122 C.E. during the reign of the Roman emperor, Hadrian, was a defensive fortification in the north of Britain. Much of the wall still stands in ruins today. The journey from Bamburgh to Whitby would have taken several days.

69. In Canonical hours, Terce is 9 a.m.

70. In Canonical hours, None is 3 p.m.

71. As previously mentioned in Etheldreda's 660 letter to Hild, Ecgfrith spent his formative years as a hostage in Penda's court, a condition of Oswiu's kingship imposed upon him by Penda. As explanation for Ecgfrith's character and personality flaws, Sneesby writes, "…the infant was taken from his mother's arms to the seat of the Mercian king, and there he stayed until Penda's final defeat and death. Thus he was brought up effectively as an

orphan and in a heathen environment, and in confronting the mood-swings and contradictions of his later years, one has to keep this disturbed childhood in mind." (*EP*, 56)

72. Etheldreda's assessment of the situation differs considerably from the Monk of Ely who claims that "Ecgfrith was enflamed with love for the virgin, and he brought measureless wealth and promised many marriage gifts." (*LE*, 1:26) Possibly, the monk was attempting to demonstrate the steadfastness of Etheldreda's resolve even in the face of such worldly temptations.

73. Eormenburga claimed to be a descendant of Ethelberht, King of Kent. (*EP*, 58–59)

74. Vespers is performed when evening comes and the lamps are lit.

75. Vigils, the night office, was celebrated after midnight; Lauds, the morning office, after sunrise, and Prime, the first hour, at roughly 7 a.m. Zero hour is considered to be 6 a.m., and all the following hours are taken from that point.

76. The Roman tonsure or hairstyle consisted of a shaved circle on the top of the head with a ring of hair around the front, sides, and back, which grows in the form of a crown. This style originated with St. Peter. The Irish or Celtic tonsure, on the other hand, consisted of the hair being shaved from the forehead back to the top of the skull. The hair at the sides and the back was left long. St. John the Evangelist favoured this tonsure.

77. According to the *Anglo-Saxon Chronicle,* there was an eclipse of the sun on May 3rd in the year 664.

78. John 13: 23 *Douay-Rheims, The New Testament of our Lord and Saviour Jesus Christ, translated from the Latin Vulgate, diligently compared with the original Greek,* hereafter identified as DR.

79. Various early writings rejected by most authorities as being of doubtful authorship and authority.

80. Geoffrey Ashe describes Irish Christianity as follows: "The Celts palpably stood for a Christianity of their own. It was not

heretical, but it was less formal and patriarchal, less tightly
administered, simpler, plainer... Poets and story-tellers, if not
priests, continued for centuries to adopt the old gods as heroes
and heroines and to evoke a world where enchantment could be
benign and even angels could be ambiguous." (*Kings and Queens
of Early Britain*, 205)

81. DR, Matthew 16:18-19

82. For a more complete version of the debates than Dreda remembers, see *HE*, III: xxv.

83. See endnote 76 for details of the tonsures.

84. Ashe, *Kings and Queens of Early Britain*, 206.

85. The plague [Parker Chronicle (A) and Laud Chronicle (E), *ASC* 664]

86. *HE*, III: xxviii

87. *HE*, IV: xxiv

88. Cædmon's hymn is the earliest surviving Old English poem. The Old English and the translation are taken from the website of Michael Delahoyde of Washington State University (public.wsu.edu/~delahoyde/medieval/caedmon.html/). Delahoyde writes that "The hymn well represents Old English poetry, with its lines of four stresses and a medial caesura, with its two or three alliterations per line, with the stacking up of epithets (God is guardian, measurer, lord, creator, master". Readers who wish to hear the beautiful cadences of spoken Old English will find a recited version of this hymn on YouTube.

89. Citing W. Bright's *Early English Church History*, 1878, p.235, Lina Eckenstein states that Wilfrid went on to build on these lands a church which was spoken of in his day as "the most wonderful building this side of the Alps." (*Women under Monasticism*, 97) hereafter *WM*.

90. Curtois, *The Conversion of the English* (107–108) hereafter identified as *CE*.

91. Some sources report these events happened while Hild was still alive. Others say it was after Eanflæd became abbess of Whitby.

92. Both the Parker Chronicle (A) and the Laud Chronicle (E) of the *ASC* report that in the year 671, "There was the great mortality of birds." No other information is offered.

93. *HE*, IV: xxxiii

94. *HE*, IV: xix

95. Bede also reports that he himself spoke to Wilfrid regarding the truth of Etheldreda's state of virginity after twelve years of marriage, and he was assured that the claim was indeed true, his proof being Ecgfrith's offer to Wilfrid of a great deal of land and money if he could persuade Etheldreda to give up her vow of chastity. (*HE*, IV: xix)

96. Curtois mentions that Æbba was King Oswy's half-sister. (*CE*, 97)

97. *HE*, IV: xix

98. Parchment, the chief material on which to write in Etheldreda's time, was highly prized for its smoothness and ability to absorb ink and because the ink could be scraped off and the parchment reused. This latter attribute was valuable because parchment was an expensive commodity. When goats and sheep were killed for meat, the choice had to be made whether the skin would be tanned into leather or left untanned and made into parchment by a long and complicated process. Parchment was particularly important to scribes in monasteries who toiled endlessly copying books. It was also used by scribes who recorded legal documents such as deeds, wills, laws for the country and agreements between parties, and for the literate nobility, such as Etheldreda and Hild, who liked to write letters. Their handwriting would, of necessity, be very cramped and would use every piece of surface. It is possible that the same parchment went back and forth between them after the ink was scraped off, creating a parchment

known as *palimpsest*. Vellum, made from calves' skin, was an even more expensive writing surface.

99. Sneesby, *EP*, 67.

100. *LE*, 1:34 and Sneesby, *EP*, 77.

101. The Monk of Ely claims that this story was attested to by witnesses. (*LE*, 1:35)

102. Ermine Street was the great north-south road built by the Romans.

103. For further illumination and conjecture regarding the traditions surrounding this miracle, see *LE*, 1:38–39.

104. Ealdwulf was the previously mentioned son of Hereswitha, Hild's sister, and Æthelric, King Anna's brother. He was, therefore, Hild's nephew and Dreda's cousin.

105. This description comes from Lina Eckenstein. (*WM*, 99) She in turn is quoting from the *History of Ely* (Bentham, 1817, 9).

106. Being aware of Hild's dislike of Wilfrid, Etheldreda has resisted mentioning that Wilfrid, as Archbishop of York, officiated at her installment as abbess. According to the Monk of Ely, Wilfrid, on his way to Rome, tarried for some time at the monastery and talked to Dreda about "things beneficial to her soul and the health of her mind." (*LE*, 1:45)

107. The Laud Chronicle (E) of the ASC for the year 672 states "Cenwalh passed away, and Seaxburh, his queen, reigned one year after him." This Seaxburh is to be differentiated from Etheldreda's sister, Seaxburga. Shortly after he left East Anglia, King Cenwalh commissioned the building of the first cathedral at Winchester, as noted in the Parker Chronicle (A) year 648

108. There are many sources for more detailed information about the life of Benedict Biscop (also known as Benet Biscop or Biscop Baducing). The *Britannia Biographies* and the *Catholic Encyclopedia* are but two.

109. Sarah Foot states that "among the finds from the excavated double house at Whitby are twelve styli and two vellum prickers, although only one surviving text is generally agreed to have been produced at Whitby: the anonymous life of Pope Gregory the Great (which now survives only in a ninth-century continental copy in the monastic library of St. Gall, Switzerland)." (*Monastic Life in Anglo-Saxon England c. 600–900*, 218)

110. *HE*, IV: xxiii

111. *DR*, Matthew 26:39, Mark 14:36, Luke 22:42

112. The seventh century memorial cross, Ovin's Stone, resides in Ely Cathedral and is the most ancient monument in the cathedral. The Latin inscription reads, "Lucem tuam Ovino da Deus et requiem Amen." The Ely writer describes Ovin as a man of amazing sanctity and great merit. (*LE*, 1:27)

113. *HE*, IV: xix

114. St. Augustine of Hippo (354–430 C.E.) is widely regarded as one of the most enduring and influential writers and philosophers of the early Western Christian church. His thinking is less revered in the Eastern Christian belief system. His feast day is August 28, the date of his death.

115. The monastic Rule of Benedict of Nursia (c. 480–550) was making its way into the monasteries of Europe and Britain in the seventh century. The Rule did not advocate extreme asceticism but rather moderation in all things.

116. Thacker, *BE*, 475

117. *HE*, IV: xix

118. The *ASC* records that the star "comet" appeared in the year 678. The Laud adds that it appeared in August and "for three months every morning shone like sunshine." (Garmonsway, *ASC*, 38) We know this now as Halley's Comet, which appears in our skies every 75 years.

119. *HE*, IV: xix

120. For a more detailed reporting of these miracles, see *HE*, IV: xxiii.

121. Once again, we can look to Bede for a more detailed description of these events in *HE*, IV: xix. See also IV: xx for Bede's hymn of praise to the virgin, Etheldreda. Curtois provides a somewhat more lurid description of Etheldreda's death and the translation of her bones in *CE*, 126–129.

122. Or possibly 710 as noted by Thacker in *BE*, 475.

123. A biography written during Wilfrid's lifetime by Stephen of Ripon may offer more insight into how he was viewed by his contemporaries.

124. Bede records the story in detail, and thus preserves in history the tarnished reputation of a woman who, by all accounts, did not deserve such condemnation. (*HE*, IV:xxv)

125. *HE*. Barnes & Noble edition, 343.

Bibliography

WORKS CITED

Ashe, Geoffrey. *Kings and Queens of Early Britain*. Chicago: Academy Chicago Publishers, 1990.

Bauer, Nancy. "Abbess Hilda of Whitby: All Britain Was Lit by Her Splendor." In *Medieval Women Monastics: Wisdom's Wellsprings*. Ed. Miriam Schmitt and Linda Kulzer. Collegeville, Minnesota: The Liturgical Press, 1996, pp. 13–31.

Bede. *The History of the English Church and People*. Introduction by Michael Frassetto. New York: Barnes & Noble Publishing, Inc., 2005.

Bede. *A History of the English Church and People*. Trans. Leo Sherley-Price, Rev. Ed. by R.E. Latham. Harmondsworth: Penguin, 1968.

Blair, Peter Hunter. *An Introduction to Anglo-Saxon England*. Cambridge: Cambridge University Press, 1970.

Curtois, Rev. H. *The Conversion of the English*. London: Society For Promoting Christian Knowledge; New York and Toronto; The MacMillan Co., 1927.

Eckenstein, Lina. *Women Under Monasticism*. Cambridge: Cambridge University Press, 1896.

Evans, G.R. *Faith in the Medieval World*. Downers Grove, Illinois: Inter Varsity Press, 2002.

Fairweather, Janet, trans. from the Latin. *Liber Eliensis: A History of the Isle of Ely from the Seventh Century to the Twelfth Century, compiled by a monk of Ely in the twelfth century.* Woodbridge, Suffolk: Boydell Press, 2005.

Foot, Sarah. *Monastic Life in Anglo-Saxon England c. 600–900.* Cambridge: Cambridge University Press, 2006.

Garmonsway, G.N., ed. and trans. *The Anglo-Saxon Chronicle.* London: J.M. Dent, 1972.

Gibbons, James Cardinal. Approbation. *Douay-Rheims New Testament Translated from the Latin Vulgate.* Rockford, Ill: Tan Books and Publishers, Inc., Photographically reproduced from the 1899 edition.

Hassall, W.O., ed. *Medieval England As Viewed by Contemporaries.* New York: Harper & Row, Torchbook Edition, 1965, pp. 14–18.

Lapidge, Michael, John Blair, Simon Keynes and Donald Scragg, ed. The Blackwell Encyclopaedia of Anglo-Saxon England. Oxford: Blackwell, 1999.

Sneesby, Norman. *Etheldreda, Princess, Queen, Abbess & Saint.* Haddenham, Ely, Cambridgeshire: Fern House, 2005.

Stenton, Frank. *Anglo-Saxon England.* 3rd edition. Oxford: Oxford University Press, 2001.

Whitelock, Dorothy. *The Beginnings of English Society.* Harmondsworth. England: Penguin, 1952.

Wilson, David M., ed. *The Archaeology of Anglo-Saxon England.* Cambridge: Cambridge University Press, 1986.

WORKS CONSULTED

Brooke, Christopher. *The Saxon & Norman Kings.* London: B.T. Batsford Ltd., 1963.

Brown, Michelle P. *Understanding Illuminated Manuscripts: A Guide To Technical Terms*. London: The British Library and The J. Paul Getty Museum, 1994.

Fell, Christine. *Women in Anglo-Saxon England and the Impact of 1066*. Clark, Cecily, and Elizabeth Williams. London: British Museum Publications Ltd, 1984.

Fisher, D.J.V. *The Anglo-Saxon Age c. 400–1042*. New York: Barnes & Noble Books, 1992.

Leyser, Henrietta. *Medieval Women: A Social History of Women in England 450–1500*. London: Phoenix, 1996.

Marsh, Henry. *Dark Age Britain: Some Sources of History*. Newton Abbot: David & Charles (Publishers) Limited, 1970.

Mitchell, Bruce. *An Invitation to Old English & Anglo-Saxon England*. Oxford: Blackwell and Cambridge, MA, U.S.A.: Blackwell, 1995.

Oman, Sir Charles. *A History of England Before the Norman Conquest*. London: Bracken Books, 1994.

Page, R.I. *Life in Anglo-Saxon England*. London: B.T. Batsford Ltd, 1970.

Ridyard, Susan. *The Royal Saints of Anglo-Saxon England: A Study of West Saxon & East Anglian Cults*. Cambridge: Cambridge University Press, 1988.

Saklatvala, Beram. *The Origins of the English People*. New York: Barnes & Noble Books, 1992.

Savage, Anne, trans. *The Anglo-Saxon Chronicles*. New York: Random House, 1995.

Sayles, G.O. *The Medieval Foundations of England*. London: Methuen & Co. Ltd., 1967.

Wilson, David. *The Anglo-Saxons*. Harmondsworth, Middlesex, England: Penguin, 1972.

Wilson, David M., ed. *The Archaeology of Anglo-Saxon England*. Cambridge: Cambridge University Press, 1986.

Yorke, Barbara. *Kings & Kingdoms of Early Anglo-Saxon England*. London: Seaby, 1990.